Acquiring Trouble

Kathleen Brooks

An *Original* work of Kathleen Brooks.

Cover art provided by Calista Taylor.
http://www.calistataylor.com

Editing provided by Karen Lawson.
http://www.theproofisinthereading.wordpress.com

Books by Kathleen Brooks

Bluegrass Series

Bluegrass State of Mind

Risky Shot

Dead Heat

Bluegrass Brothers Series

Bluegrass Undercover

Rising Storm

Secret Santa, A Bluegrass Series Novella

Acquiring Trouble

Relentless Pursuit

Secrets Collide

Acknowledgment

Thank you to Mrs. O for taking the time to teach me about PTSD in our soldiers. There are so many wonderful organizations providing care to our men and women in service. I encourage everyone to learn how you can help.

As always, thank you Chris, Milo, Marcia, Craig, Karen, Jan, and Calista for your hard work. I am thankful to have such a wonderful team of people to work with.

Prologue

Keeneston, 17 years ago…

Miles Davies leaned against the wall and took a sip of beer out of the red plastic cup he held. He glanced around at the people dancing in the living room of his best friend's house as the band played. His friend, Josh, was currently shirtless as he pounded away on the drums while playing some Green Day song.

It seemed as if this memory would live in his mind forever. He couldn't believe he had just graduated from high school and soon everyone in the room would be drifting off all over the country. Josh was off to the University of Louisville while he was going down to Texas A&M at the end of summer—hopefully not alone.

Miles looked up from his beer to see the breathtakingly beautiful blonde in a tight white dress, pearls around her neck and wearing cowboy boots, sauntering toward him. Her perky breasts bounced and drew his attention as a braless Stacy Thomas, the captain of the cheerleading team, approached him.

He ran his hand over shoulder-length brown hair and pushed a stray lock behind his ear. Stacy stopped in front of him and shot him a smile that went straight to his groin. She reached her slender hand out and took his red cup from him. She wrinkled her nose at the smell, but took a drink anyway.

"I don't know how you men can drink this stuff."

"It's an acquired taste, babe."

"I know what I have a taste for, but I can't get it here in the middle of a roomful of people," Stacy's perfectly pink bottom lip stuck out slightly as she pouted. Miles felt her eyes roaming his body and he responded instantly.

"I can go see if Josh's room is empty while your girls steal you away from me." Miles kept one eye on a group of cheerleaders making their way to their captain. "It's the last room on the right. Come find me when you're done. There's something I want to ask you about so don't let them keep you too long." He leaned down and captured her lips in his. He plunged his tongue into her mouth just long enough to have her leaning into him. There. That should hurry her up.

Miles smiled at the gaggle of girls now surrounding their leader and headed down the hall, past the keg, and into his friend's room. It was quieter down here and gave him the privacy he needed to gather his courage. Stacy had been accepted to Vanderbilt University's pre-med program. It's where her father had gone and where she was expected to go too. She was going to be spending the summer shadowing her father at the hospital. Miles was hoping that three years of dating was enough to sway her from that path.

He took a deep breath and put his hand in his pocket to finger the small thin promise ring he had bought her. He was going to ask Stacy to transfer to Texas A&M so that they wouldn't have to do the long-distance-relationship thing. He'd already looked at apartments for them both and knew she'd say yes if he asked. She had hinted at it many times over the past couple of weeks.

The knock on the door caused his breath to catch in his throat. He had never been so nervous! He watched as the doorknob turned and a big black boot appeared. He looked up in confusion and saw the pale white skin, ink black hair, and vibrant violet eyes of Morgan Hamilton. Great, just what he needed. The bad girl of Keeneston was probably trying to sneak a smoke or take a swig of vodka in privacy before vandalizing the room. Who knew what she wanted, but it probably wasn't good.

He had once thought Morgan was nice, even pretty. But that was before freshman year. Morgan's sister had wasted no time in showing everyone how little she thought of Morgan when she started high school. Her sister had been the cheerleader captain then, and between their dislike and Morgan's subsequent behavior it was clear she wasn't the type of girl Miles would ever go for.

She only wore black and she had dyed a streak of her hair purple. It matched her eyes perfectly, but he doubted she cared. Thick eyeliner coated her eyelids and drew attention to her eyebrow piercing.

"Morgan? Do you need something?" Miles asked her. He glanced at the clock; Stacy would be here soon and he wanted Morgan out before she arrived. Stacy hated Morgan more than any person in the world. "Morgan, what are you doing here?" he asked again when she just stood there staring for a moment.

He saw her take a breath and then walk all the way into the room, closing the door gently behind her. She looked up and pinned him with her eyes. The violet shade darkened and he couldn't help but momentarily get lost in them.

"When faced with the probability of everyone going away to college or jobs outside of Keeneston, it seems as if tonight gives us a certain freedom to say and do things we've always wanted without fear of embarrassment or ridicule at school on Monday morning," she said confidently as she walked closer to him. Her voice was lower than Stacy's, but seemed to weave a spell around him.

"I suppose." Miles felt his brow furrow in confusion as he watched this little imp stop in front of him. She barely made it up to his chest, but few women did. He was six two and his cowboy boots made him even a bit taller than that.

"I have to tell you something," Morgan paused. "Thank you," she choked out.

"For what?"

"You were always kind to me, even when others weren't. You helped me study for that math test sophomore year when no one else would be my study partner and you never pretended I was invisible. I really appreciate that. You were the only one who did so."

"You know, more people would've been kind if you showed your true self and didn't hide behind this rebel, bad-girl attitude... and appearance." He scanned her baggy black cargo pants, ratty Nirvana t-shirt and dark purple fingernail polish.

"Appearance doesn't make a person!" Morgan said as she placed her hands on her hips and stared him down.

"See, that's why people weren't nice to you. You're so short and defensive with people. Maybe if you acted more like your sister..."

"Oh! My sister—the freaking saint! I could never live up to her. No one could! Tell me, Miles, would my sister do this?"

Morgan grabbed his shoulders and pulled him down before he could even realize what was happening. Her lips, purple lipstick and all, were on his kissing him hard. He was shocked. Shocked by the fact that he liked it. Shocked when her aggressive tongue pushed into his mouth. Shocked that he felt full breasts against his chest and a hand sliding down to cup his growing erection. He couldn't help himself. He closed his eyes and lost himself in her intoxicating touch.

Morgan couldn't believe her boldness. But the man of her dreams was alone in the room and had compared her to her sister. It was the only way she could think to prove she wasn't her saintly sister—she was better. The fact that Morgan had been dreaming about this moment for four years contributed too.

She moaned into his mouth as she felt his tongue slowly move in response to her kiss. The turmoil of the last four years melted away. The fight with her parents and sister just this afternoon left her mind and was replaced with the permanent memory of the feel of Miles's tongue in her mouth and the weight of his erection in her hand. She ran her other hand across his muscled back and slid it around his shoulder, bringing him closer to her.

"Oh my god!" someone shrieked.

"Dammit. Babe, it's not what it looks like. She kissed me," Miles tried to explain to an outraged Stacy.

"So is she the reason you're going to Texas and didn't even apply to Vandy? To be with this skank?"

Morgan felt her eyes go round, her hands clenched into fists. She was used to being called names, but that didn't mean it didn't hurt.

"I would never be with someone like her, you know that. You're all that matters to me," he pleaded.

Morgan ducked her head and pushed past Stacy and into the hall. People were staring at her and whispering as she ran past them. Once out in the night air she ran as fast and hard as she could. Anger filled her. Her feet took her to the back of the hardware store on Main Street. She looked around, approached the back door, and quickly picked the lock.

Two hours later Morgan was high above the town with a can of red paint. She stepped back from the tower and leaned against the rail. "Miles Loves Morgan" was written in huge letters across the side of the water tower facing town. She signed his initials under it and then pulled out the note she had written and a strip of duct tape. She attached the note where it would only be visible to someone standing where she was and then climbed down.

Morgan picked up her two bags that sat in the field and walked away from Keeneston forever.

Chapter One

Miles sat in his office in Lexington and read the document in front of him. It was a warm night, but he had been in his office so much recently he forgot it was even the beginning of fall.

He loosened his dark red tie and slid his black suit coat off, hanging it on the back of his chair as he stood up with the papers. He paced across the office reading them one last time. He paused in the middle of a long stride when he heard the soft knock at the door.

"Come in," he barked. He looked up at his quiet assistant, Claire Montgomery, as she made her way into the office holding a sheet of paper. "Is that the final agreement?"

"Yes. The Kentucky Restaurant Council just sent this over via courier. It's signed by the president. They approved your initiative. All 300 plus restaurants belonging to the council have agreed to purchase local produce from our farmers! Isn't that wonderful? The farmers are going to be so excited."

Claire was a middle-aged housewife turned assistant. He hired her because she had raised triplet boys. They were now in high school and during her interview she had joked that she needed the job for the bottomless pits that were teenage boys' stomachs. He figured anyone who could control three teenage boys could handle anything.

Miles smiled as he looked at the signed agreement for his company, Family Farms. During college he had discovered that the heart of farming, the small family farms like his parents', were being run out of business by large corporations which then bought the failing farms for pennies on the dollar during foreclosure.

These corporations were negotiating huge contracts to supply their produce to certain governments, restaurant chains, grocery stores, and more. They lobbied Washington to keep quotas on farmers based on the size of their farms or the produce they were generating.

Miles started his company with the intention of being competitive with the large corporations. He pulled in family-owned farms from all over the state under one umbrella. Instead of three hundred small family farms competing for sales independently, they combined their power and growth into one organization. It resulted in being more competitive for contracts such as the one he just closed with the Restaurant Council and the one for the regional grocery store he was currently in negotiation with.

"I just got this email from Top Producers, LLC," he said as he handed it to Claire. "They wanted to congratulate me on getting the Kentucky Restaurant Council contract. If you read it you'll see where they are supportive of our cause but I believe they are fishing."

"What would they be fishing for?" Claire wondered as she leaned over his shoulder and read the email.

"Us. I'll bet you anything they are interested in finding out if we're weak enough to be taken over. David Washington, the president of Top Producers, will come in and garner support for a change in management, then once in power he'd break up and dismantle Family Farms faster than you can blink. Without us here, the farms will slowly go bankrupt. I'm sure David is counting on that. He's done it before and I can't see that he would suddenly want to help the local farmers."

"So, how are you going to handle it?" Claire absently fiddled with her belt as she worried. His secretary was loyal to a fault. Her parents were both farmers and she took it as her personal mission to look out for every client of Family Farms as if they were her own family.

"It means more long hours. I need to find a way to make us look invincible to the investigators so they'll tell David to save his money and go after someone else."

"Mr. Davies, you already put in long hours. You need to take a break," she worried.

"I can take a break later. I need to strengthen our defenses—closing on the grocery deal will help, because this is going to be a battle. David will take a couple months to investigate and that gives us time to develop a plan of action."

"Do you want me to stay and help?" Claire asked.

Miles looked down at his watch and grimaced. It was already past seven and Claire had a family at home. "No thanks. I'll get started and then we can go over my ideas on Monday." As Claire left, Miles thought about calling his brother Marshall, the Sheriff of Keeneston, and seeing if he needed help with the dog-fighting ring he was tackling. He'd give him a call right after he pulled some info on last quarter's sales.

Miles ran a large hand over his face and stood up to stretch. He looked around his office and realized it was dark outside. He glanced at his watch and cursed as he saw it was five in the morning. He'd done it again. This whole week had been a blur. He spent his business hours on the phone with the farmers discussing crop yields, talking to banks, and lining up potential contracts. Nighttime was the only time he had to work on the grocery store proposal because his days were filled with fortifying the company.

It shouldn't really matter that he wasn't sleeping. It wasn't like he'd slept since that night in Afghanistan when Cade had been captured. That was almost six years ago now. Surely his body was used to getting the three hours of sleep a night he relied on.

He welcomed the late nights. When he did go to bed early, it wasn't like he actually went to sleep. He subconsciously prevented himself from going into a deep sleep. He was always on alert. Always listening and evaluating every noise he heard. At least this gave him something to do when he was lying in bed at home wide awake.

Miles went over to his chair and slid his suit coat on. He patted the pockets and pulled out his cell phone. He had turned it off when he visited with some of the farmers and hadn't bothered to turn it back on. He grabbed some files and picked up his keys when his cell phone beeped. He dug it back out of his pocket and looked at the screen. He had three missed calls and two voicemails. One was from his brother, Cade, and two were from his mother.

He locked up his office as he listened to his brother's voicemail first and then his mother's. Apparently Marshall had found the dog-fighting group and arrested a huge number of people. Their brother-in-law, Cole Parker, who was with the FBI, was helping out along with the DEA.

Miles looked at the timestamp of the last missed call and saw that it was just an hour ago. Marshall was probably still on scene wrapping everything up. He'd check with his brother, get a couple hours of sleep, and then get some more work done all before he was due at his mother's for dinner.

He had gotten a lot done this past week. He had received positive news from many of the farmers and was almost done with the grocery store proposal. He was waiting for his contacts to get in touch with him when one of David's men called for information on Family Farms. He was sure they'd be checking out every business deal where his name was mentioned.

Miles took a deep breath of the early morning air. Lexington was still asleep. The offices in the historic downtown were dark and the normally busy streets were empty. He opened the car door, placed his wrinkled suit coat on the seat next to him, and went to check on Marshall.

Morgan Hamilton was in the middle of a lovely dream about running her own company. She was at the head of a long table with her employees around it. They were all facing her and listening to her morning briefing before she sent them out to conquer the world.

Her very own executive assistant came into the room with a stack of papers. He opened his mouth and all that came out was a ringing noise. The man tried again to tell her something and again all that came out was that annoying ringing sound.

Morgan groaned and without lifting her head from her extra-fluffy pillow she slowly reached her perfectly manicured hand out from under her comforter. She didn't bother to open her eyes. She'd find the blasted ringing cell phone in just a minute. Morgan felt her hand hit the nightstand and slapped around until she felt the phone. She grabbed the phone and pulled it under the comforter before putting it to her ear.

"This better be good," she mumbled.

"It is. Now get your ass out of bed." Morgan's eyes shot open as she bolted upright on the bed at the sound of her boss, David Washington.

"What's going on?"

"I need you to start an investigation for me. Tad found a company he thought might be a good prospect. I've looked over the surface material, newspaper coverage, and so on and think it has potential for a takeover," David snapped. He never sounded nice and it was particularly grating so early in the morning.

"Why isn't Tad doing the investigation?" Tad was an ass-kisser and David loved to pit them against each other.

"Oh, Tad wants it and he'll get it if you screw up. But the company is over in Lexington, Kentucky. You're from Kentucky, aren't you?" her boss asked with his constantly disapproving voice.

"Yes, I grew up close to Lexington. I know the area well."

"Good. That's why you have the lead. This has potential to be a big deal. I want to know everything about this company—financials, the ones on the record and the ones hidden. I want to know their standing in the community, who each member is, and what they grow. I want to know what the president of the company eats for breakfast and what the table he eats it on is worth. Assets, debts, deals in the works—I need all of it."

"That's going to take a while, David," Morgan told him as she typed notes into her tablet.

"I know it is. Just do it right. I need to have all my ducks in a row for this one. Then we'll see if you can actually close the deal," David sneered. She could feel his squinty eyes over the phone.

It didn't matter that she had been doing just that for five years at Top Producers. David was still surprised she managed to drive herself to work through DC traffic in the morning, let alone actually close a deal. He was just a prick. There was no other way to put it.

"Of course I can. What am I working with?" Morgan asked as she took more notes.

"The company name is Family Farms. It's this co-op type business. Pain in the ass is what it is. Just took the Kentucky Restaurant Council contract from us. All the farmers are members in the LLC. The president of the LLC negotiates contracts on the farmers' behalf in order to compete with companies like mine. I sent the bastard an email congratulating him. I'm sure it would make him suspicious if he had half a brain, but he's nothing but a redneck. I need all the info you can find."

"I can do that. What do you think it's worth now?" Her fingers flew over the tablet as she tapped in her notes.

"Twenty million. The by-laws require the president to take any offer to the farmers who hold a stake in the company. My guess is the majority will agree to allow him to negotiate the best deal he can on their behalf… or reject any such deal. The best is to stop him from getting that majority. If you can't, then work directly with the president. Depending on what you find out in your investigation, I'll give you authority to go up to thirty million if you need to. I want that company, one way or the other."

Boy, today was going to suck for David's executive assistant. It was Sunday at five in the morning and she could feel his blood pressure rising over the phone. She started a new section in her notes as David ranted about no-good stupid farmers with crops for brains.

"Who's the owner and what do we know about him?"

"A tight ass named Miles Davies." Morgan's head swam as the sudden image of her high school crush crashed upon her memory. "I can't find out too much on him besides that he went to Texas A&M and graduated with a B.S. in Agricultural Studies. Then he went on to Purdue to get his MBA in Agricultural Management. Immediately upon graduation he enlisted in the Army. When he got out he started this company. That's all I got on him. I couldn't get anything out of what he did in the Army or where he served. Although, I guess it doesn't matter. A nerd like that would be placed in some command center to play with his computers and files."

A nerd? No, Miles' wasn't that. Yes, he was smart. But you could never look at a man like that and think all he did was shuffle files. Even at just eighteen he was more of a man than any of the men she'd dated since. There'd been lawyers, doctors, financial advisors, a personal trainer, and even a very flexible yoga instructor with better hair than hers. Still, Miles always eclipsed them. The memories faded as the years passed, but the feel of that kiss never did. She'd dream of it only to be awoken by him telling her he would never date a girl like her. Now here she was in a luxury condo with a sports car and no one to wake up with. No one to share it with.

"Morgan! Morgan, is there a problem? Do I need to hand this over to Tad instead?"

"No David. I'm fine. I was just taking notes." She refocused on her tablet and took a calming deep breath, taught to her by the flexible yoga instructor, to clear her mind.

"Good. I want you to get started on this immediately. And Morgan…"

"Yes?"

"You better make this happen."

Morgan placed the phone on her nightstand and flopped back down on her bed. Why did the mention of his name turn her into a scared self-conscious teenager again?

Chapter Two

Miles had followed Marshall to the dirt turnoff that led to his home in the early morning hours after Marshall wrapped up the crime scene. His brother was doing a terrific job as sheriff. Miles made a quick sandwich and sat in the leather chair overlooking the farm. The large windows glowed as the sun rose over the rolling hills of the countryside.

Miles finished his sandwich and rose to check the locks on all the doors and windows. He set his alarm system and climbed the stairs to his bedroom. He knew every creak of the floorboards, every background noise from the air conditioner or refrigerator, and every sound that was out of ordinary. His house was still and quiet, and that was the way he liked it.

He entered his room and locked the door before taking off his suit coat and tossing it on the upholstered chair. He yanked his tie free, strode across the room stripping his shirt off, and flipped on the bathroom light.

A large glass shower took up the majority of the brown and cream tiled sidewall. He unbuckled his belt and freed the button of his slacks before turning on the hot water. Miles pulled his cell phone and wallet out of his slacks before stepping out of them. The shower was the one place where he felt he could relax. He had had multiple showerheads installed. A glass door and the large window in the bathroom allowed him a view of his farm.

Miles opened the glass door and was about to step in when he heard his phone vibrate. It was probably his mother reminding him of family dinner. For each of his thirty-six years they had family dinner every Sunday night at six. Yet, every Sunday morning for the past six years his mother called him. "This is your mother," she'd say, as if he didn't already know. "Remember we have dinner tonight at six. Don't be late." It was usually followed up with, "dress nicely, we have a guest coming," which meant his mother had found a date for him. Some mothers knitted, some baked, but his mother hunted for potential brides.

"Yes," he snapped when he saw a number he didn't recognize. He was tired, naked, and just wanted to get into the hot shower.

"Um, Mr. Davies?"

"Yes, what is it?" The mumbling scared voice only confirmed his suspicion this was probably someone wanting to know his views on the upcoming election or some garbage like that.

"I'm calling on behalf of Top Producers."

"Again, what is it?"

"Please hold for a call from Miss Hamilton."

"Fine. But hurry up, will you?" He was naked and starting to get cold, which made his shower look even more inviting. Boring music flowed through the phone as he waited for Miss Hamilton.

"Miles, dear, what a coincidence that you're the president of Family Farms!" A woman's voice floated across the line. She had a confident voice with the cutest hint of a southern accent.

"I'm sorry. Do we know each other?" Miles ran through all the people he knew at Top Producers that he'd met at conferences but couldn't place her.

"It's been a while. Seventeen years or so. But I still remember you. What does the Keeneston water tower say now?"

Miles didn't blink. He didn't breathe and his heart practically stopped beating. Not Miss Hamilton—Miss *Morgan* Hamilton! "Morgan."

"Is that all you have to say after the way we parted?"

"Well, if you're giving me a call on behalf of Top Producers then it can't be out of the goodness of your heart since we both know you and goodness don't go together."

Morgan's laugh sent a tickle through his ear as he waited for her response. "Miles. Your dry sense of humor is still intact after all these years. It was so very attractive when we were in high school together."

"Stop with the pleasantries. What can I do for you?" He didn't know what it was, but he was sure it wasn't good.

"Smart as always. David told me he sent you an email of congratulations and while he doesn't know you, I do," she said smoothly.

"Don't presume to know me, Morgan."

"Play nice, Miles. I know that when you got that email you knew we were interested in learning more about your company. You have a nice little thing going. Congratulations."

"Little? So little we're starting to win the contracts Top Producers is bidding on. Look, Morgan, I appreciate you not tip-toeing around the subject. You want to take us over."

"You're getting a little ahead of yourself. I'm just telling you that you're doing well enough to warrant us taking a look under your skirt to see if we like what we find."

"Since you're an old friend, I'll save you some time. We don't lift our skirt for just anyone and certainly not you. Good luck finding as much as you can about us, 'cause I won't give you a thing. And if you manage to be good enough to find the information, I'll give you a heads up. We won't sell. There will be no takeover. You all try to dress it up and call it a merger—either way, it's not happening."

"Well," Miles could hear the smile on her face, "I look forward to trying to sneak a peek under your clothes. It's been great talking to you, Miles. I'm sure we'll talk again once I complete the investigation."

"Forgive me for my lack of manners, but I hope I don't hear from you again. I will fight this and so will my members. Goodbye, Morgan."

Miles placed the phone on the counter and walked to the shower. Stepping under the spray he was assaulted with visions of the past. Visions of a slightly overweight girl with raven hair, mystical violet eyes, and baggy black clothes… of the girl that kissed him graduation night with such abandonment he still got hard thinking about it.

Stacy had walked in in the middle of a kiss that had left him so hot he would've taken Morgan against the wall before he even realized what was happening. Her lips had set him on fire, and her touch had almost undone him right then and there. Stacy had shrieked and the spell had been broken.

Morgan bolted and he had been left with one pissed-off cheerleader. Not that he was surprised. He was utterly and completely at fault. He could've stepped away. He could've prevented her from kissing him. But he didn't. He had apologized and taken responsibility.

Stacy was crying and he had never felt worse. He begged, pleaded, and promised anything he could to get Stacy to stay with him. Finally, in the early hours of the morning Stacy had forgiven him. She had the promise ring on her finger although she wasn't moving to Texas A&M right away. The vice around his heart had eased as he drove her home.

He smiled as she slid her hand onto his leg and leaned over to kiss his neck. He turned down Main Street and suddenly her hand wasn't being so gentle. She had gasped, and then pummeled him until he stopped the car.

"What the…"

"You bastard! You said it was a one-time thing, but it's not, is it? How long has this been going on?"

"Stacy, calm down. What are you talking about?"

"That!" Stacy pointed toward the sky. Miles had looked to where she was pointing. There, in bright red paint was Morgan's artwork.

"I didn't do that!"

"It has your signature on it. And, you had red paint on you yesterday." Stacy accused.

"I was painting a barn, you know that."

"No, I don't know that. That's it. It's over. My father warned me about you. I should've listened." Stacy shook her blonde hair and stared out the window.

"Warned you? About me?"

"Yes. He knows I'm going to join the Belles and said you didn't quite come up to snuff. After all, you're just going to be a farmer. I need to go to Vanderbilt and keep my options open."

"You're right. That's exactly what you need to do." Miles started the car up and drove the remaining couple of blocks to her house. He watched as Stacy got out of the car, "Good bye, Stacy. Good luck finding the perfect man for you."

Miles stopped his car outside of his parents' farm and looked around for unknown cars. His mom was starting to get smart and would pick "the guest" up or have her park behind the house. He thought about checking, but he was honestly too tired. After he had gotten out of the shower he had climbed into bed, but sleep had evaded him.

Hopefully Marshall was here tonight. He needed a moment with him to talk about Morgan. Miles had never told anyone what happened that night. He hadn't wanted to hurt Stacy or Morgan so he just kept his mouth shut. One night in the desert of Somalia, however, he had told Marshall what really happened. Marshall was the only one who really knew how much of an effect that kiss had had on him and now he needed Marshall.

He didn't need many things. He was the oldest of the six Davies kids and was responsible for keeping his eyes out for his siblings. But, now he really needed to talk to Marshall.

Miles took the stairs two at a time and hurried into the house. Looking around he saw that it was just family and Marshall wasn't here yet. His sister-in-law, Annie, was talking baby stuff with his sister, Paige. They were both looking very round as they finished up their seventh month of pregnancy. He couldn't wait to be an uncle. He'd spoil them rotten.

"Son, how are you doing?"

"I'm fine Dad." Miles nodded to his dad and took the beer he offered. His father, Jake, was a tall quiet man. His brown hair had started to gray. Most of his sons looked just like him.

"I know you've taken your role as big brother seriously, but if there's something bothering you, you know you can come to me, right."

"Dad, nothing's bothering me." Miles turned to the sound of the front door opening and saw Katelyn Jacks and her family enter.

"Well, just remember what I said." His father gave him a pat on the back before walking away.

Miles watched as Katelyn, a former model dressed perfectly with her long blonde hair put up into a sleek ponytail, made the rounds. He worried that with her here he wouldn't be able to talk to Marshall. He really liked the new veterinarian, but Marshall tended to have tunnel vision when she was around.

After talking to Katelyn's father about a possible deal between his hotels and the farmers, Miles was feeling like his old self. This could be his second biggest account and would strengthen Family Farms for the war he was sure Top Producers would wage.

Finally he saw his brother sneaking into the house. He excused himself from talking about the bust with Cole and intercepted Marshall before he got across the room to Katelyn. But, it was to no avail. Tunnel vision had set in. Between Marshall's preoccupation with getting to Katelyn and their mother calling for dinner, Miles decided not to bother him. Clearly Marshall had other matters on his mind. Miles would just take care of it himself just like he'd taken care of everything and everyone else in his life… by himself.

Chapter Three

Miles stopped his car at the gate to his property and stepped out to undo the chain. He checked the piece of clear tape he kept on it to see if it had been opened while he was gone. After scanning the horizon for movement and listening for out-of-place sounds, Miles returned to his car. Old habits from the war were hard to break.

He had a medium-sized pond between the gate and the house filled with geese that honked if they were bothered. The geese lifted their heads and honked in welcome as he drove by. He checked the motion sensor that was hidden in the tree line to make sure the detectors weren't obscured. A small red light was blinking so he stopped the car. That meant something had set it off.

He opened the trunk of his car and pulled out a sniper rifle. He clipped on the night scope and started a systematic scan of his property. Through the green lens he saw a deer munching on the berry bush, a possum chilling in a tree, a dog sitting on his front porch, and a herd of cows munching on the grass… wait, a dog on his porch? He didn't have a dog. He was not a pet person.

Miles finished his scan and determined the stray dog had set off the motion sensor. He drove up to the house and parked his car in the garage. Miles walked slowly toward the small dog trying to determine if it was friendly. The dog looked like a corgi mix with a really long tail. He had a gray face, black nose, tan hair with dark brown ears, and a white chest. His legs were short and stumpy. When Miles looked into the dog's sad brown eyes, all he could think about was this dog had an old soul. Something tugged at his heartstrings when the dog sat up on his hind legs and waved at him.

"I guess you expect me to let you into the house and take care of you, huh?" Miles smiled when the dog batted his big lashes and gave a little yip. "Okay, but only for tonight." The dog thumped his tail and followed him inside the house.

Miles undressed and lay down in bed after checking all the door and window locks. He set the alarm, but turned off the motion sensor with the dog in the house.

He shut his eyes and a pair of violet eyes danced before him as he drifted off to sleep. In his dream he was kissing Morgan again all those years ago. Then the shot rang out. Morgan's eyes widened as she fell to the ground. When he looked up he was no longer at the graduation party, he was in the mountains of Afghanistan.

Afghanistan, six years ago…

Morgan was gone and he was looking through his scope at his brother, Cade. He was behind a large rock with a shoulder rocket launcher ready to disable an approaching caravan of terrorists. Their intel told them that the middle car in the three-car caravan held the daughter of the Secretary of State who was kidnapped while her college archeological group dug for Bronze Age artifacts near the Afghanistan and Tajikistan border.

Miles and Cade had been sent in as members of the elite Delta Force on an unsanctioned mission to destroy the terrorists and rescue the hostage. Cade was to take out the first truck. Miles was to take out any terrorists that came out of the third truck while Cade reloaded the rocket launcher to take out the third vehicle. Then they'd converge on the second vehicle and rescue said hostage.

Miles trained his scope on the road and watched as two covered trucks and one Subaru WRX STI appeared on the horizon. The covered trucks probably carried supplies, guns, or rebels. The beast of off-road racing, the Subaru, was probably where Mariah Brown was being held. He signaled to Cade who readied the launcher. Miles gave one last sweep of the area and stopped at the rocky terrain beside Cade. Something bothered him, but he couldn't tell what it was. He slowly scanned the area and then saw it. A slight reflection of the sun off a scope caught his attention.

"Cade, we have company," he said into his com.

"Where?"

"The rocks. 300 yards to your right."

"How many?"

"I don't know. I only saw one with a sniper rifle."

"What do you want me to do?"

"Hold on." Miles scanned the area as the caravan approached and detected more movement. Men with automatic rifles and machine guns started to get into position.

"I count eight men. All with automatic weapons. Abort. Abort. I think we were set up."

He watched as Cade turned quickly and fired into the rocks. The explosion was violent and took the eight terrorists by surprise. Cade turned and ran for the rocks that hid Miles. The caravan slammed on the brakes and men spilled out of the back of the trucks.

"Shit! You got twenty men on your tail. Move dammit!" Miles took a deep breath, let it out and began to pick off the terrorists one by one. "Dump the launcher, it's slowing you down."

Miles changed the clip and a hail of gunfire erupted around him as they tried to pinpoint his location.

"Man approaching on your left flank," Miles told Cade as he took out the man on Cade's right.

Cade had pulled out his pistol and fired on the men, but they were coming too fast now. Cade was taken down hard. Miles fired when he was sure he wouldn't hit Cade and watched as his brother fought for his life. He was helpless three hundred yards away as Cade was hauled to his feet and beaten by the ten remaining men.

Miles watched as a battered and bleeding Cade surrendered. He looked right at Miles and winked his swollen eye as much as he could. It was their sign for the remaining team members to fall back, regroup, and then attempt a rescue mission when and if they were able. There was no way that was going to happen. He'd rather die than leave his brother behind.

He looked around the rocky terrain and gauged the best way down the hill without being detected. Shouting drew his attention back to his brother. One of the men had pulled a pistol out of his holster and was pressing it against Cade's head. The man was quickly losing his temper as Cade refused to talk.

Miles felt as if the world slowed on its axis. He moved without conscious thought from behind the rock. With the rifle secure against his shoulder he fired as he ran down the slope. His feet slid on the loose rock, but all he could see was the gun pressed against his brother's temple. He took down man after man who made the mistake of not diving for cover.

Miles slowed as he came within twenty-five yards of the man who had hauled a now unconscious Cade in front of him, using him as a human shield. There were only three of them left now. Two behind a rock and then the lead man holding Cade hostage.

"Let him go," Miles shouted in Dari.

"Release an American spy? You'd have to kill me first." The man grinned and tightened his hold on Cade.

"You made your choice." Miles fired without hesitation, hitting the man in the forehead.

He released his hold on Cade who fell to the ground. Before he could run to his brother's side the two men emerged firing at Miles. One laid cover while the other ran for Cade's body.

"No!" Miles shouted as he ran forward firing his weapon. He never felt the bullet that ripped through his bicep or the one that tore through his side. All he could see was the still, bloody heap of his brother lying lifeless on the gravely ground.

Miles's eyes shot open as he woke up screaming. He sat up so quickly that he knocked the dog sitting beside him off the bed. He was wet, drenched in sweat. His throat was raw from screaming in his sleep from another nightmare. He heard the dog whimper and look nervously at him.

"Did I scare you?"

The dog stepped back from the bed and took a running jump to get onto it again. He nuzzled Miles's arm and licked his face.

"Oh, so this isn't all sweat. You were licking me, trying to wake me up, weren't you?"

The dog thumped his tail and rested his head on Miles's lap. Miles found himself calmed by the simple act of petting the dog. He looked over at the clock—three in the morning. Well, at least he got three and a half hours of sleep tonight. That was an hour more than yesterday.

"Well, if you're going to stay with me you need a name," he said as he continued to pet the dog, feeling the adrenaline slowly leaving his system. It would take him a couple of hours to recover from this. "Bill. You look like a Bill." The dog thumped his tail in approval.

Miles got out of bed and pulled on a pair of black boxer briefs. Bill followed him down the stairs and over the dark hardwood floor to the living room. Leaving the lights off, Miles took a seat in the leather chair and looked out the wall of windows at the farm. Bill curled up at his feet and was snoring within minutes. Miles settled in and waited for the sun to come up. He hadn't missed a sunrise since that day he rescued Cade.

Chapter Four

Christmas Eve…

Miles smiled as he dropped the signed contract for Jacks Hotels in the mailbox. He had followed up with Katelyn's father after Marshall and Katelyn had gotten engaged and had won the contract to supply food for restaurants in every Jacks Hotel. Miles was still in tight negotiations with the grocery chain over who would supply the fresh produce, but he was sure with this new contract in hand he'd be able to best Top Producers and have Family Farms produce in the stores by summer.

Miles hadn't heard a word from Morgan and had actually managed to forget about her long enough to realize he wasn't thinking of her. It was a vicious cycle that he was hoping to end with his trip to Germany. He was on his way to Wright-Patterson Air Force Base in Dayton, Ohio to catch a cargo transport to Ramstein Air Base in Germany. He had boxes and boxes of Christmas gifts to give to the wounded soldiers that his farmers and the townspeople of Keeneston had put together.

He hadn't been to Ramstein since he was a patient there. Miles didn't know how he'd handle going back, but he knew how those soldiers felt being injured and so far from loved ones. When his old commander told him donations were down this year, he knew he had to act. His sister, Paige, and sister-in-law, Annie, assured him the babies weren't due until after Christmas so he had agreed to go. He just hoped he didn't miss too much while he was gone.

Morgan placed the final report on Family Farms on David's desk and waited for him to look up. It was Christmas Eve and she had come in on her day off to finish up the report. She had turned over every stone, looked behind every filing, and used up every favor she had to find out more about Miles's company. And she had found it. It was all sitting there in the file on David's desk.

"So, what do you think?"

"Family Farms is stable, growing, and a very sound investment. I'd purchase it in a heartbeat. It could easily turn into the most profitable acquisition Top Producers has ever made." If she wasn't trying to take the company over, she'd have told David how proud she was of what Miles built. He was running a very successful company that was doing well for the farmers of Kentucky.

"Good. I'll look over it. Get to Kentucky as soon as the holidays are over and start working on the acquisition." David pushed the file aside and Morgan realized she had been dismissed.

She glanced down at her watch and realized if she hurried she could reach the airport in time to catch her flight for her vacation. She was just happy she could finally take a break. It had been a year since her last day off and she liked to do anything she could to forget about work over the holidays. This year she was on her way to Fiji. She'd spend her Christmas vacation on the beach with a cocktail in one hand and a good book in the other. Morgan had scheduled her return for January 2nd, knowing she'd drive to Keeneston the second she arrived back in DC. But for now she was going to focus on forgetting work and the hazel eyes that haunted her dreams.

Miles smiled as he thumbed through all the pictures he had taken of Paige's son, Ryan, and Cade's daughter, Sophie, since his return from

Germany. He couldn't believe the call he had gotten from his mother early Christmas morning. She was so happy she couldn't stop crying, and if he was really honest with himself, he was jealous of Paige and Cade.

When little Sophie wrapped her tiny hand around his finger, he felt his heart growing. Then Ryan had grabbed his nose and cooed and it grew even more. He'd never thought of himself as a family man, but he wished he could find someone to start a life with. He just knew he wasn't going to tell his mom he was looking!

Miles had also managed to make it back to Keeneston before his brother Cy left. It was so good to see his brother. He knew Cy missed being at home and was so glad he was able to be here to meet Sophie and Ryan. Miles had spent the holidays with the entire family and loved every moment. But now it was time to get back to work and there was no better way to start back on the grocery contract than by eating some of Miss Violet's country ham and cheese grits.

Morgan leaned over the steering wheel of her car to get a closer look at the farms surrounding the road as she drove into Keeneston for the first time in seventeen years. She slowed her car as she approached Main Street and took a deep breath. It felt surreal to be back in her hometown.

She noticed all the little things that had changed, but it still seemed like the same old town. Christmas lights were still wrapped around all the lampposts making the town glow. A new bench was placed in front of the library. Mr. Simmon's antique store was now an insurance agency with the name of one of her classmates over the door.

People still walked the streets and waved to her, even though they couldn't see who was behind the tinted glass. A large tractor drove down the street and the smell of sweet feed from the Horse and Feed Store tickled her senses.

It looked like Main Street had had a makeover recently too. The historic brick buildings were painted in shades of tan, yellow, blue, and deep reds. The window trim was freshly painted white and made the large rectangular windows pop against the painted brick.

Morgan looked around and then pulled into the courthouse parking lot. She grinned at the memory of climbing up one night and riding that horse statue in front of the courthouse until Sheriff Red made her get down. She was placed in the back of his car, her second home, and taken back to her father and mother. Since her father was the sheriff's minister, she tended to avoid most arrests. Most of the time she just got a ride home and had to endure one of her father's lectures until sunup.

She turned off her black Mercedes and looked across the street at the Blossom Café. She could see the people in the plate glass window eating breakfast. Oh, she was going to have some fun this morning. Payback was a bitch.

Morgan looked farther up Main Street and back to the café. It appeared that it was still the only place to eat in town. It might have the only thing she missed from Keeneston—the pecan pancakes the Rose sisters made.

Morgan pulled out her purse and applied some lip-gloss. When she returned the visor to its place, she saw a curvy woman in a dark green suit and camel pea coat with beautiful auburn hair waving madly out on the sidewalk.

"Who is that?" Morgan asked herself. She looked around to find out who the woman was waving at. No one was near, so Morgan assumed she must have been waving at her. She could have been from high school. It wasn't like she had remembered everyone after all these years. Could it be Stacy? That huge rock on her hand made her someone's wife.

Morgan opened the door and slid out in her black pencil skirt and amethyst silk blouse. She put on a matching fitted blazer and took one last look around to make sure she was the only one there and then turned to the woman who had now stopped waving.

"Oh! I'm so sorry! I thought you were someone else," the woman laughed. "There's only one person in Keeneston with a car like that. I take it you're lost."

"No," Morgan answered as she slid her oversized black sunglasses up and onto her head.

"Well," the woman smiled again. She really was a peppy sort of person. "I'm McKenna Ashton, but everyone calls me Kenna. Do you need help finding anything?"

"Ashton? As in Will Ashton?" Morgan asked as she snapped her eyes back to the woman.

"Yes. I'm his wife." Kenna answered, a little hesitantly now.

"You're not from here and you're not Whitney," Morgan said, almost accusingly.

"Thank god for that." Kenna retorted with overwhelming sarcasm.

Morgan grinned. This woman had spunk. She hadn't liked Whitney either. She had been in the same charity group with Whitney in DC, but hadn't seen her for a while. She'd also never let Whitney know she grew up with Will. Not that Whitney would care. Morgan just liked to hear her rant about her husband's hillbilly home. She didn't like to admit it, but every once in a while she got homesick and it was nice to hear about Keeneston.

"At least Will got rid of her. I couldn't stand that ditzy blonde act." Morgan slid her sunglasses back in place and started to walk toward the café.

"I'm sorry, I didn't get your name?" Kenna called after her.

"Morgan. And it's so nice to be back." She tossed a tight grin over her shoulder and headed across the street. She had a town to shake up.

Daisy Mae Rose tapped her pen against the counter inside the Blossom Café as she waited for her sister, Violet Fae, to finish the biscuits and sausage gravy for John Wolfe's table.

"You got ants in your pants?" Violet asked as she poured the gravy over the large buttery biscuits.

Daisy rolled her eyes, "Come on already, will ya?" She tapped her pen some more since she knew it got on her sister's nerves. Finally her sister put the plate down on the counter and Daisy grabbed it. The smell of the homemade biscuits and sausage gravy made her stomach rumble. She'd never admit it, but her sister made the best breakfast.

Daisy headed to the front of the café where John sat by himself. It would be the perfect time to get caught up on the entire town's gossip. No one knew more about what was going on in Keeneston than John. As she arrived at the table Daisy glanced out the large front window and paused with the biscuits and gravy midway to the table. "Oh my heavens!" she gasped.

"Daisy Mae, what is the matter with you? Put the darn biscuits down on the table!" Violet called from the kitchen.

Everyone turned and looked at Daisy and then followed to where she was looking. Pam Gilbert, the PTA president, stood up, smoothed her khaki slacks and straightened her pink polo shirt. She excused herself from the fundraising meeting and stepped over to the window with the rest of the café patrons. Across the street she saw a woman in a black suit talking to Kenna.

"What in tarnation?" Pam leaned forward for a better look. "Holy bologna!"

"Well slap me silly and call me Sally," John Wolfe murmured as he stood up to join Daisy and Pam at the window.

"Move over, let me see," said Noodle, one of the Keeneston sheriff deputies, as he peered over Pam's shoulder. "Holy Mackerel. I need to call the sheriff, 'cause here comes trouble."

"For the love of Pete, someone tell me what's going on." Violet yelled with her ever-present wooden spoon in her hand.

"Morgan's back and coming this way!" Daisy shouted back, causing the rest of the café to gasp in unison. Some people eyed the back door and the people crowding the widow scattered.

"Morgan? *The* Morgan?" Tammy asked as she shoved her way to look out the window. "Shut the front door!"

"Good idea!" Daisy hurried to bolt the door of the café.

"Miss Daisy, it's just an expression."

"Oh, well, it was still a good idea," Miss Daisy mumbled.

"What do we do?" Noodle asked, his eyes widening in panic.

"Get it together! You'll probably have to arrest her." Miss Violet said from the safety of the kitchen.

"What on Earth is she doing here, Pam?" Daisy asked.

"I don't know." Pam shrugged her shoulders and stared as the woman approached the café. "But we're about to find out."

Morgan approached the café and saw the faces behind the window scatter. Some things never changed. She wanted to make a splash and this was the best way to do it. All those years away she wondered how many of them thought she was in jail. They probably just hoped she'd never come back, but trouble had just returned to Keeneston.

She opened the screen door and then pushed open the door. The smells that wafted over her were delicious, but it was the silence that caught her attention. She looked around and noticed some familiar faces. The Rose sisters looked exactly the same. John had gotten rounder and Noodle had turned into a man—a nervous man at that. Morgan removed her sunglasses and smiled at the roomful of people. The smile didn't reach her eyes.

Morgan watched as Pam approached her. Pam had aged. Her dirty blonde hair had turned brown. She looked so much older. Morgan supposed the same went for her, but at least she hadn't turned into someone resembling a stick-in-the-mud like Pam had.

"Hello, Morgan," Pam said as she stepped in front of Morgan.

"Hello, sis."

Chapter Five

Morgan looked into the blue eyes of the sister she hadn't seen in seventeen years. Morgan hadn't returned for her wedding thirteen years ago. It was the one time she had called home randomly. Her mother answered and let it slip that Pam was getting married. The phone was snatched away by her father who told her in no uncertain terms that she was not to return home and ruin her sister's day. No one wanted her there to put a dark stain on Perfect Pam's perfect day.

They didn't have to say it, she knew why. They were afraid she'd steal the groom away like they thought she did with Pam's last boyfriend. In fact Morgan had heard from Whitney about Pam's two boys. Apparently they had made too much noise at the café after a soccer game one night. Whitney bitched about it at the next meeting. All the society moms nodded and talked about how hard it was to find a good nanny.

"What are you doing here?" Pam asked in a cold tone she inherited from their father. Morgan was actually surprised Pam would even acknowledge her.

"Don't worry, I won't intrude on your town for long. But you better lock up your husbands and boyfriends just to be safe." Morgan smirked and held some dark satisfaction when Pam's face paled.

"I'll ask again," Pam said in what Morgan could only describe as a Mom voice, "what are you doing here?"

"I'm in town for business and to have some pecan pancakes." She looked at Miss Violet who only grunted in acknowledgment of the breakfast order, but refused to move from her spot behind the counter.

Morgan turned when the front door flew open and hit the wall. Miss Lily stumbled through the door with her white hair on end and her broom in her hand. She looked around and then went to stand by Miss Daisy.

Pam turned back to Morgan and looked her over. "What kind of business are you in?"

"Yea, it must be good if that's your car." Daisy nodded out the window to the Mercedes.

"Yes. It is. I'm Director of Mergers and Acquisitions at Top Producers in Washington DC," she said with pride. They were all looking at her with interest now. The bad girl had gone corporate instead of to prison.

"What does that have to do with Keeneston?" Pam asked accusingly.

"I believe she's here to see me. Isn't that right Miss Hamilton?" Miles stood from his seat in the back of the room and buttoned his dark gray suit coat.

Morgan was momentarily stunned. He had grown another inch at least. His body had filled out and matured even more. His shoulders were wide and thick. His eyes were a dark hazel and no longer held the spark of innocence and youth. He was handsome as sin and Morgan couldn't help but remember the kiss. Her eyes went to his lips and then dropped lower. My, oh my, had he grown up good.

"That's right Mr. Davies." Morgan smiled seductively and sauntered to the table as the whispers rose around her. She heard the words *Stacy, breakup,* and *water tower* as she stopped in front of him and smiled.

Miles had been trying to eat his country ham and cheese grits when all hell erupted in the café. He didn't need to get up and look out the window with the rest. He knew why Morgan was here and what she wanted. She had completed the investigation and found out just how strong his company was and wanted it. What he wasn't expecting was what he felt when he saw her.

She was no longer the chubby girl hiding behind baggy clothes, although she still had a penchant for dressing in black. But the black suit she was wearing accented all her curves, and boy were they some curves. Her breasts were supple. The purple silk shirt clung to their roundness and enhanced them in a way that made him sit up and take notice.

Her skirt was tight and high waisted, showing off how her slim waist flared out into her rounded hips forming a perfect hourglass figure. Her violet eyes dared anyone to challenge her as she announced her return to town. Her eyes gobbled him up as she approached him, never once looking away, then stopped in front of him.

"Should I kiss you hello?" Morgan asked him. His groin tightened at the thought even though it was made in jest.

"Once was enough, thank you."

"Still holding a grudge?" she laughed. "I'm sure Stacy has forgiven you and that you're blissfully happy with your two kids and dog." Miles detected the tightness in her words even with the smile on her face.

"Stacy dumped me after your water tower stunt. She went to medical school at Vandy, met and married a fellow doctor. However, I don't think my dog gives two tail wags that you're here." It still hurt when he said it. He had loved Stacy with the passion only a teenager could.

"Well, it looks like I finally lived up to my reputation."

Miles tightened his square jaw and narrowed his eyes at her. "Why don't you meet me at my office in an hour and we'll talk business then," he said as he tossed some money on the table.

"With pleasure, Mr. Davies. It'll give me time to enjoy the delicious pancakes Miss Violet is whipping up." She pulled out the chair across from him, "I'll even take your seat since you're leaving."

Morgan didn't watch as Miles stalked out of the café. She sat down in the chair and took a deep breath. Her back was to the café and she hoped it would signal them to leave her alone. There was only so much pretending she could do and she needed time to regroup before negotiations started with Miles.

She reached into her purse and pulled out her smartphone. Morgan started to respond to her email even as she felt Perfect Pam take the seat Miles had just vacated at the small round bistro table. Morgan ignored her. They'd talked enough for one lifetime that night seventeen years ago. There was nothing left to say.

"Morgan?" Pam asked quietly. "Where have you been for the last seventeen years?"

"Here and there," she responded, never looking up from her email.

"What our parents did was wrong, Morgan." Pam whispered.

"As I recall it, it wasn't just our parents." Morgan looked up when Miss Daisy set the plate of pancakes in front of her. "Thank you." Miss Daisy grunted and walked off as Morgan took a bite.

"Morgan…" Pam began.

"Look, Pam. I'm going to eat my pancakes and go to my meeting. I won't disturb Perfect Pam's perfect life. You leave me alone and I'll leave you alone… just like it was growing up," Morgan spat.

"That's not what I want. Not now. Morgan, where are you staying?"

"At a hotel in Lexington."

"Oh no you're not." Miss Lily said as she put her hands on her hips. "Come hell or high water you're a Keenestonite and you'll stay here in Keeneston with your family."

"Is there a new five star hotel I don't know about?" Morgan asked in her most superior voice.

"Don't sass me, missy. You'll stay at the bed and breakfast and that's the end of it." Miss Lily wiggled her finger at Morgan and she could feel her temper rise.

"Funny how things have changed. Seventeen years ago you kicked me off your property and even threatened to call the sheriff if you found me in your yard again, and now you want me to stay with you? Thanks, but no thanks," Morgan said snottily.

"Morgan, you owe it to your family to…" Miss Lily started, but Morgan had enough. She stood up, effectively cutting Miss Lily off.

"With all due respect, my family disowned me along with the rest of this town. I don't owe you or them anything." Morgan spun on her heel and walked out of the café letting the door slam behind her.

Trouble had definitely come back to town and she was going to do everything in her power to make them feel her wrath. They had turned their backs on her and now they were going to pay. She was going to take Miles's company and enjoy every minute of ripping it apart as he sat and watched along with everyone else in town. It may not affect Keeneston directly, but she'd show them she wasn't some young delinquent to be ordered around anymore. Nope, she was a woman in charge and Miles was about to find out just how in charge she really was.

Chapter Six

Miles slammed his car door and took a deep breath. What was it about Morgan Hamilton that got him so worked up? He had tried to put her out of his mind from the second she broke that kiss on graduation night. She was nothing but trouble to him, yet it was her memory that haunted him along with his nightmares of war.

He had gone to college and thought he had fallen in love. But, when he kissed her it was Morgan's eyes he saw and her mouth he tasted. That was the ironic part. It was only one kiss in high school and he still wasn't over it. When he joined the Rangers he took his time off base seriously and tried to erase Morgan's memory with the women who frequented the bars around Fort Benning, Georgia. It hadn't worked and he had grown more and more frustrated.

When he joined Delta Force, he didn't have time to think about women. He was just trying to stay alive. He had gone on countless dangerous missions and had frozen his emotions. He showed no fear, no anxiety, no hate, no love. He was the team leader and with that he was responsible for bringing back every member of the team. He forgot about love, lust, and happiness.

It had worked. He only lost one team member in the four years he was on duty. However, the day that Cade was taken a crack appeared. He had fought it, but it was there. Miles had been asked to stay on for another four years, but he knew he couldn't pretend anymore. He had lost the edge he depended on. That cold calculation he used when dispensing the enemy.

Miles enjoyed the corporate world – the negotiations and the team mentality of supporting the farmers in the state. However, even he knew he was having problems. He hadn't slept in years. He hated to sit with his back to doors. When entering a building he always looked for escape routes and sniper positions. Certain smells and sounds would also send him flashing back to those mountains and Cade being held hostage.

So, to avoid the dreams and anxiety he found himself thinking about Morgan. She was never going to come back into his life again and that made her safe to think about. To build a story around, to relive that kiss, her hand on his manhood without any consequences. No chance of a messy breakup. No sleepless nights worrying about trying to explain to a woman why he didn't sleep. But now she was here and feistier than ever. Not to mention hotter than ever. She was so voluptuous. He wanted to explore every inch of her. Instead he had to break her down and toss her out. She was trying to take his company and he couldn't allow that.

Miles started the car and began the short drive to Lexington. He had Claire gathering as much background on Morgan and Top Producers as she could before the meeting, but he needed more. Marshall was usually his go-to guy for hacking computers, but he was preoccupied with planning his wedding just a couple months away in March. Well, he did have more than one brother with a talent for internet snooping. Miles picked up the phone and punched in the number.

"Cade, it's Miles. Do you have a minute?"

"Sure. This is my planning period so I have forty-five minutes." Cade was not only the football coach at Keeneston High School, but also taught biology and other science classes there.

"Thanks. Are you by a computer?" Miles told him about Morgan and Top Producers as he drove the winding road.

"No problem. Give me just a minute to look her up. I can't believe Morgan is back. I bet the café was crazier than all get out." Miles heard Cade pounding away on his laptop. "Phew," Cade whistled. "This girl has done a lot in a little time."

"Like what?" Miles asked. The Morgan he knew in high school wasn't the go-getter type.

"No arrests, not even a parking ticket, which is amazing considering parking problems in DC. She lives in an upscale condo complex—alone. Has a gym membership that she uses sporadically. Seems she really liked yoga, but stopped taking classes a year ago. She's in multiple charitable organizations. Wow, didn't see that one coming. She helps animals, kids, and old people. This doesn't sound like the girl I've heard stories about," Cade said between typing.

"What happened after she left Keeneston?" Miles asked as he pulled onto Main Street in Lexington.

"She was admitted to Georgetown. She graduated in three years while working part-time at a lobbying firm. Upon graduation she earned her MBA in one and a half years and scored a very lucrative position as a lobbyist on Capitol Hill. She regularly lobbied Congress and even had a couple of meetings with the President. She worked there for six years until Top Producers came calling.

"She entered as an associate and on track to make partner. She was promoted two years ago to Director of Mergers and Acquisitions where she has taken over, broken apart, and rebuilt eight companies under the Top Producer's brand. Geez bro, I think you may have met your match."

"Thanks for the vote of confidence, Cade." Miles said sarcastically as he pulled into his reserved parking space. He heard his brother chuckle as he hung up.

Miles read over the report that Claire had handed him upon arrival. He shook his head as he put the last piece of paper down. Top Producers were only interested in buying up companies and destroying them. They overtook them, pushed out the controlling parties, and fired all the employees. In the case of farms, they made deals outside of the best interest of the owners of the farm so that the farmers couldn't fulfill the contract. Most of the farmers put out a lot of money up front on equipment in order to fulfill huge contracts.

In almost all of the cases Top Producers loaned that money and held a lien on the equipment. They also went to the banks and took over the mortgages on the farms. When the farmers failed to fulfill the contract they didn't get paid and couldn't cover the payments on the equipment. It would landslide and soon they couldn't cover the mortgage. Top Producers would go in and force a quick foreclosure. The farms would be bought by a subsidiary of Top Producers for pennies on the dollar.

Miles' intercom buzzed and he knew he had only a couple of minutes before Claire brought Morgan in. He put the folder away, smoothed down his shirt and tightened his tie. Morgan walked in with her briefcase and glanced around the room before stopping before his desk.

"Good to see you again, Miles."

"I wish I could say the same. Let's make this meeting quick and to the point. I'm not selling. Tell David he wasted money in sending you here." Miles leaned forward in his chair, not bothering to get up. This was going to be short.

"Now, we haven't seen each other in all this time. I think we should chat a little before you reject me again." Morgan unbuttoned her suit jacket and sat in the chair opposite Miles. "Besides, I know that as soon as I give you our proposal you'll need to take it to all your members. So it looks like we're going to have a lot of time to spend together." She smirked and leaned back in his leather chair, slowly crossing her stocking-clad legs.

"Let me guess, you're going to do everything possible to prevent me from getting the signatures needed to reject whatever the offer is, probably pay them off, buy their votes," Miles accused.

"Why would you say that? I've done nothing to make you accuse me of breaking the law, not to mention the ethics of business." Her purple eyes flared even though her voice remained calm, almost teasing.

"Probably because you were a constant law breaker and you work with David Washington, a felon in a suit. You wonder why I question you? That night after graduation is enough to make me question you." Miles sat back in his chair and watched a blush creep up her face.

"You don't know what happened that night any more than you think you know about me. You know the saying about assuming…"

"I don't need to assume, the whole town knows exactly what type of person you are and what type of deals you'll probably make and then break." Miles had had enough playing. She was tormenting him with her straight-laced appearance and attitude, yet he knew what passion hid under that suit. Regardless of lust, he wasn't going to let her walk all over him to close a deal that would hurt his fellow farmers.

"Oh," Morgan whispered as she ducked her head.

Miles watched as she slowly raised her eyes and looked at him from under her dark lashes. She slowly licked her bottom lip with her pink tongue before nibbling on her lip with her teeth.

"I'm so sorry I ever gave that impression. I always work *hard,* very *hard* for what I want," Morgan said breathily as she put her hands on his desk and slowly stood up, leaning over toward Miles.

Miles felt his heart speed up and his pants tighten. He couldn't help but lean forward to get closer to her. She was spellbinding. He couldn't take his eyes off of her as she gently bit down on one red nail. He watched in anticipation as she slowly trailed that one perfect red nail over her plump lip, down her sweetheart chin, and between the valley of her full breasts.

Morgan closed the gap and brushed her lips against his with a feather-light touch. With a growl that came from an animal long caged, he grabbed her with a frenzied passion. His lips melded to hers as he wrapped one strong arm around her waist and pulled her across his desk and into his lap. She was kissing him back with the same intensity that she had all those years ago, but she had learned a trick or two since that inexperienced kiss.

Her hand yanked his shirt from his pants. She was breathing heavily, her breasts pressed against his chest, his erection yearning for her touch. His breath caught as he felt her fingers dance slightly along his waistband. Morgan broke from the kiss and leaned forward to trail her lips along his masculine jaw to his ear.

"I thought I'd give you what you expected from me," she breathed into his ear as she ran that perfect nail over his length, "Maybe you even expect me to sleep with you to close the deal—because I'm nothing but a criminal who lacks ethics and who liked to shoplift packs of gum when I was a kid."

"Geezus Morgan!" Miles leapt up, dumping Morgan onto the ground. "That is exactly what I was talking about. Some people never change and this… this was completely inappropriate."

Morgan just smiled from where she was sitting on the ground. Her skirt pushed up to her thighs allowing her black garters to peek out. She stood slowly and straightened out her clothes. Damn her, she didn't even look a bit as frustrated as he felt.

"Your assumption of knowing me is what is inappropriate. I just had a little fun showing you how your little assumptions are going to lead to your downfall. Now, I have some farmers to talk to. I'm sure they'll be real happy to learn of our offer of fifteen million dollars." Morgan picked up her brief case and looked back at Miles. "Good bye Miles. It's been titillating as always."

Miles watched as she lowered her eyes to his pants and he cursed under his breath as she gave a little smile at the evidence of just how titillating of an experience it had been. With a quick shrug of her shoulders she turned around and left him staring after her in a lust-filled haze. He wasn't quite sure, but he thought she might have gotten the best of him.

Miles rocked backed on his heels and smiled. It could possibly be one of the first real smiles he had had in a while and it felt good. This was going to be the most satisfying business negotiation he'd ever had the pleasure of winning.

Chapter Seven

Morgan held her back straight as she marched out of the office, down the stairs, and out to her car. She started the car and managed to drive two blocks before she burst into tears.

The second she left Keeneston that dark night seventeen years ago she ceased to be the Morgan they had known. Instead she was a good student, a hard worker, a valued employee who wasn't only law abiding, but also donated her time to charity. She was a respected member of the community.

Then in the course of two hours she had been reminded of every horrible thing she did—abandoning her family, even though they had disowned her, breaking up the relationship of the town's golden boy, and then told she lacked ethics and was a criminal. That's why she never came back to Keeneston. Away from here she could be her real self, because if she were her real self in Keeneston they'd eat her alive, just like seventeen years ago.

Keeneston, seventeen years ago…

Morgan tossed her graduation cap into the air along with the rest of the class and watched it join in a cloud of blue and white caps. She had done it. She had graduated and today was her eighteenth birthday. She was legally free to do whatever she wanted and what she wanted was to get her own place, live her own life.

It didn't start out that way though. She had loved her parents and her sister. When she was young there were so many happy times. After turning seven years old it all changed. Her hair, which had been a light brown like her mother and father's, had darkened to the black it currently was. Her blue eyes had turned violet when she was four and for some reason her father looked at her sitting across from him at the dinner table and exploded.

She didn't understand it, but from that moment her mother detached from her and focused all she had on Pam. Pam had taken her cue from their parents and stopped being nice to her. She was suddenly a burden to the teenager instead of the best friend she used to be. Her father barely tolerated her presence and came down on her hard whenever she got into trouble. When she was good he just ignored her, so over time she learned that if she wanted his attention she had to be bad. So she'd lift a packet of gum or knock over a trashcan. But now, it was over. Now she was graduating and now she'd be her own woman.

Morgan reached up into the air and plucked her cap from the sky. Her classmates were surrounded by their parents and other family members and friends. She stood alone on the outskirts of the groups and watched alone. She had told her mother that she was going over to a friend's for lunch, but it was a lie. She didn't have any friends.

She took off her cap and gown and started the short walk home. She was hoping to sneak in through the kitchen, grab a bite to eat, and hide out in her room until everyone went to bed. Then she was going to leave forever. She looked up at the innocent looking house and dreaded having to go inside.

Morgan saw Pam's car in the driveway—of course Pam had a car and she didn't even have a bike. Great. It was her birthday and graduation, but with Pam here she could forget anyone even remembering. She cut across the well-manicured lawn and entered the screened-in porch. She opened the door, stepped into the kitchen, and came face to face with her family.

"What are you doing here?" Pam shot at her. "Mom, you said she wouldn't be here!"

"Morgan, we're having brunch with Pam's boyfriend, Stephen. You were supposed to be busy. I don't have enough food for you," her mother told her.

"You need to respect us and not embarrass your sister. Leave now so we can enjoy our meal." Her father stood next to Pam as they glared at her.

Morgan didn't even pay attention to Stephen. He looked like any of Pam's typical boyfriends. Average. Average height, average build, average looks. Morgan just thought of him as boring. With a shrug of her shoulders she headed outside and sat on the porch. She'd wait until they moved into the front living room and sneak in. It shouldn't take more than thirty minutes.

She was curled up against the wall with the warm sun coming in through the leaves. The breeze was moving the trees gently and before she knew it she was sound asleep. Sound asleep until she felt someone kissing her. Her eyes flew open to find Average Stephen sitting next to her giving her an average kiss and with his average hand roaming up her leg. Morgan slapped him hard and he just smiled and shoved her hard against the house.

"I heard you were naughty and I know how naughty girls like it," he growled into her ear. She opened her mouth to cuss him out when he shoved his tongue in it instead.

"Oh my God! Morgan! How could you?" Pam shrieked, causing Stephen to fall back.

"I'm sorry, muffin, your sister just came onto me. She was teasing me and a man can only take so much. Then she just kissed me."

"That's not true! Pam, I would never…"

"Morgan, get out of my house at once! I will not tolerate such behavior. I've had enough!" her father yelled as he stood with his hands on his hips and his face red.

"Fine! I never want to see you again!" Morgan screamed back as tears threatened to spill.

"I believe the feeling is mutual. I wish you were never born! You've ruined my whole life!" Pam shouted before running inside, the screen door slamming behind her.

Morgan couldn't stand it. Her father was kicking her out, her sister wished she was never born, and her mother just stood quietly in the corner of the porch, her hands twisting a napkin between her thin fingers. Morgan looked at her for help, but her mother just kept her head down.

Morgan shoved her way past Average Stephen and ran down the stairs and down the street. She hid behind Miss Lily's large pink rose bushes. That's when she knew what she needed to do. She'd sneak into her house from Miss Lily's side. Her bedroom window was there and she could jimmy it open, grab the money she'd been saving up and make her way to DC. She'd talk her way into a job on campus and one way or another find a way to get into the dorms early.

She waited for another couple of hours until Average Stephen left with a blotchy-faced Pam next to him. As she approached her bedroom window she listened for her parents. She heard yelling and knew it was about her. She removed the screen and pushed up her window. Morgan looked into her room and was relieved to see the door shut, but with the window now open she could hear more of her parents' argument.

She climbed in through the window and grabbed her large duffle bag and backpack. Morgan lifted the lamp in her room and pulled out the tight wad of money she had been saving and tossed it into her backpack along with her personal items. She grabbed a bunch of clothes and tossed them into her bag. She froze when she heard her father's voice rise.

"No, I don't think I was too harsh on her. She's a jezebel, just like her mother."

"Please, don't take my mistake out on her. Take it out on me, don't make her go."

It was the first time her mother had stood up for her to her father. But why was he calling her mother names? Her mother was the most passive creature she'd ever seen—not like her, that's for sure.

"She's the product of your sin with another man. She bares his mark and she bares your loose behavior. I won't have her darken my doorway one more time. She will not ruin the happiness of my true daughter any longer. She is banished from this family and I'll tell her so when she dares to show her face again."

With the slam of a door she heard her father leave. She finished throwing her clothes into her bag and quietly walked to the formal living room. Her mother stood, broken and crying in the middle of the empty room.

"Mom?" she asked in a way that conveyed all the emotions rolling through her.

"You heard?" Her mother bowed her head and with a deep breath looked up at Morgan. "I can tell you did."

"Is it true? Is Dad not my father?" Morgan managed to whisper.

"Yes, it's true. He agreed to raise you and be your father, in return I was to stay his wife and never tell anyone the truth. Although, anyone who looks at you should be able to tell you're not his. You look nothing like him or Pam. But, your father just told everyone you were the spitting image of his grandmother and everyone thought that was so special." She shook her head in disbelief.

"Who's my real father? When? How? I don't understand?"

"We were at a conference nineteen years ago. There was this man, he was there with his wife. We fell in love and it just happened. We started an affair. After one week of knowing each other, we knew we were soul mates.

"We parted at the conference and stayed in touch. He was from Cincinnati and we talked on the phone every week. He told me he was going to leave his wife and I decided to take Pam and divorce your father." Her mother started shaking and Morgan wrapped her arms around her. She was so frail. It was as if life had beaten her spirit down.

"So, why didn't you leave him?"

"I did," she said quietly. Her eyes glazed over as she went back to that time. "I had the car loaded, Pam was in the car seat and we were preparing to go to Lexington to file divorce papers. I had found out I was pregnant that morning. The phone rang. I thought it was him and I couldn't wait to tell him about you. Instead of it being him, it was his brother-in-law, informing me that my love had been in a car accident. He had died and his wife wanted to invite us to his funeral."

Morgan's heart ached for her mother and a father she would never know. There was also relief. Relief that the man who had either ignored or berated her wasn't her father. Relief that she wouldn't end up like him.

"Your father found out. He threatened to tell the whole town about me and kick me out without a dime…and, and that he'd take Pam from me. If I stayed with him and never mentioned it again, he'd raise my child as his own and I'd get to see both of my children grow up instead of just one. I had to stay. I couldn't risk losing either of you."

"Come with me, Mom." Morgan grasped her hands.

"Where?"

"I have a full scholarship to Georgetown University. Grab a bag, we'll go together."

Her mother took her hand in hers and squeezed it. Silent tears fell from her cheeks. "It's too late for that. I've made my bed, now I must lie in it. But it's not too late for you. Go and live. You're so bright and talented and I am so proud of you."

Morgan collapsed into her mother's arms and cried. Her mother loved her. All this time, she was just trying to give her a life. She had just discovered her mother, how could she leave?

"I can't leave now. Not with learning all this. I feel like I just found you. How can I leave you now?"

"You must, baby. He won't let you stay. He'll destroy you like he has me. But," her mother pushed her back and looked into her eyes, "we don't have to say goodbye forever. Your father is always working on his sermons from three to five every Saturday. Call me then. Let me know where you are and how you're doing. I can't believe my baby got into Georgetown!"

Her mother reached for her again and crushed her to her chest. Morgan felt the tears that she had buried release. Her mother soothed her as she felt wave after wave of tears pour out of her.

"Here, honey. I want to give you something." Her mother hurried away into the laundry room and returned a couple seconds later. In her hand was a silver necklace with a black onyx horse with a long tail and proud head.

"What's this?" Morgan asked as her mother laid the necklace in her hand.

"Your true father gave it to me. He loved Morgan horses. This was a replica of his horse. That's how you got your name—to remind me of your father every time I heard my husband say your name. I'm sure that was wrong of me, but it's what got me through the years. I couldn't show you affection, but I felt it. Please, please say you'll forgive me." Her mother's frail hands grabbed hers with more strength than Morgan thought was possible. She felt something else placed in her hand and her mother squeezed.

"Of course I do. Is it bad to say that I'm relieved? So many things make sense now."

"I'm so sorry I didn't tell you earlier. I should've left all those years ago, but I'm not as strong as you are. You better go before he comes home. Here, take this." She removed her hand and Morgan looked down at the large wad of cash.

"Mom? Where'd this come from?"

"Every week my husband gives me money for household things. I took a fourth of it and put it aside to save. I want you to have it. I want you to do all the things I ever dreamed of. Education, travel, independence—you have all the makings of a strong woman and I know you'll succeed because you've never backed down. Promise me you never will."

"I will, Mom. I'll never let anyone put me down."

Morgan kissed her mother and picked up her bags. With one last look over her shoulder she walked out of her house. As the darkness fell she stashed her bags in the large rose bushes next to Miss Lily's house and headed to the graduation party. She told her Mom she'd never back down and the first step was to tell Miles how she felt before catching the bus to Washington DC.

Morgan dried her tears and put the car in gear. It was time to go visit her mother again. She drove to the cemetery in Keeneston with a heavy heart. She had called her mother every Saturday at 3:30 for the next eight years. They had a relationship that was closer than any mother and child could have, and all in secret.

Then one Saturday she had called and Pam had picked up the phone. Morgan recognized the voice, but Pam had not. When she asked for Mrs. Hamilton, Pam tearfully told her she had passed away in her sleep last Saturday afternoon. Apparently after their last talk she had gone to take a nap and never woke up. The funeral was to be the next day after a service in her honor.

Morgan had driven home, hidden in the back of the church and let the anger harden her even more. Her "father" hadn't shed a tear. He was a peacock preening under the attention. When the service moved to the cemetery she had followed far behind. She had stepped into the old cemetery and hidden behind a huge maple tree. Only after everyone had left did she go to her mother's grave and grieve. She laid red roses against the headstone and, with her hands, dug in the fresh dirt as she sat on her knees. She took off her necklace and placed it in the hole before covering it again.

"Now you two may enjoy peace and happiness, together," she whispered to her mother.

As she stood over her mother's grave now, she looked at the spot where she buried that necklace and knew that her mother was happy. Never back down. Well, she sure as hell wasn't going to do that now, even for the only man she'd ever loved.

Chapter Eight

Kenna handed the last gift to Katelyn as Paige readied herself to take notes. Katelyn ripped into the large heavy gift and everyone oohed and aahed at the appropriate time.

"Thank you for the frying pan, Miss Violet. Gosh knows Marshall doesn't have too many of these lying around."

"Well, dear, they're good for keeping him in line too. A man might not remember you naggin' at him, but he sure remembers a smack to the head with a frying pan." Miss Violet folded her hands neatly on her lap as the other ladies surrounding her nodded in agreement.

"I never tried a frying pan, I always, accidently of course, dropped a horseshoe on Beauford's foot," Katelyn's grandmother, Mrs. Wyatt, responded in her slow Georgian drawl.

"Well, a woman's gotta do what a woman's gotta do." Miss Daisy said as she started to pick up empty cake plates.

"Oh fiddle dee, put that down Daisy Mae. This is my house and you're not cleaning up my granddaughter's wedding shower. Now sit down a spell and enjoy yourself."

"Well, now that the shower is over and most of the people are gone, I have something I want to know about," Kenna said as she took a seat next to her best friend, Danielle De Lucca Ali Rahman, who became the princess of Rahmi when she married Mohtadi Ali

Rahman, or Mo to everyone who knew him. Dani had just found out she was pregnant at Christmas, but wasn't yet showing.

"Oh! Gossip, do tell," Katelyn giggled as she too joined the circle.

"Don't start without us!" Paige Davies Parker shouted from the other side of the room along with her similarly baby-toting sister-in-law, Annie Blake Davies. Little Sophie and Ryan weren't quite three weeks old yet and were enjoying being fussed over at their first outing.

"Well," Kenna began, "Last week when I was in town a black Mercedes pulled up at the courthouse. I thought it was Dani or Mo, and so I waved and waited for you to get out. Only, it wasn't you."

"Who was this impostor?" Dani teased.

"Some woman with black hair and eyes so dark blue that they actually appeared to be violet. She looked like Elizabeth Taylor and with the diva attitude to match! Who is she?" Kenna asked.

"She's my sister," Pam said as she sat down with a glass of Rose sister special iced tea.

"I never knew you had a sister." Kenna leaned forward along with Dani, Annie, and Katelyn. Paige however, just scowled.

"I haven't seen her for seventeen years now."

"Too bad it couldn't have been another seventeen," Paige sneered.

"Paige! I've only heard you talk that way about Kandi and her sultry ways. What's this person ever done?" Katelyn asked as she took a tiny sip of the tea. She'd learned her lesson about the Rose sisters' drinks. They were potent.

"She destroyed Miles's life!" Paige exclaimed.

"She wasn't very nice or good growing up," Pam's motherly voice cut in, "She had a crush on Miles and kissed him on her last night here. His girlfriend walked in and saw it. She broke up with him because of Morgan. It seems Morgan ruins whatever she touches."

"Geez Pam, that doesn't sound like you either. What is it about her that makes people who are so open and nice talk so harshly?" Kenna shook her head and looked from Pam to Paige.

"She was a bad apple," Miss Lily put in. "She stole little things from the store, she vandalized some properties with paint, knocked over trash cans and so on."

"She pierced her eyebrow and dyed her hair purple," Miss Daisy added.

"She tortured my father by acting up constantly. She wore my mother's nerves out. She not only broke up Miles and Stacy, but she made my boyfriend break up with me too. Then she just up and left graduation night and was never seen or heard from again until she waltzed back into town last week. She never even came back for my mother's funeral or my father's when he passed a few years later," Pam explained. "But, my parents were very hard on her. Now that I'm a mother, I see that maybe they were a little too harsh on her. I just don't know, can someone really change?"

"I've been thinking the same thing," Miss Lily shook her head, "I yelled at her and hit her with my broom that night when I caught her messing with my roses before she left town. I don't know what's she's been doing all these years, but she appears to be very successful, even with a big chip on her shoulder."

"And, every year on the date of my mother's death, there's a fresh bouquet of red roses placed on her grave," Pam told them.

"Do you think it's Morgan?" Dani asked, getting more into the legend of Morgan.

"I don't know. I don't know what to think or how to handle having her back in town," Pam shrugged.

"Well, you may be in doubt, but I'm not. Miles was heartbroken over losing Stacy. I don't know if he ever recovered. He certainly hasn't had any long-term relationships since then." Paige scowled as she rocked Ryan to sleep in her arms.

"I think she sounds interesting. Maybe I just need to get to know her. You know, one bad girl to another," Annie laughed.

"Pish Posh, you're not bad!" Miss Lily smacked Annie's leg and Annie just laughed.

There was a lot about her life that no one knew. She had a feeling she and Morgan would get along great.

Miles hung up the phone and raked his fingers through his hair. In two weeks Morgan Hamilton had swayed thirty of his farmers to her side while he only convinced twenty-three. He wasn't used to losing, and he wasn't going to this time, even if he couldn't stop thinking about grabbing that long black hair and wrapping it around his hand as he pulled her head back for a blazing kiss that would leave her quivering.

Bill howled and Miles opened his eyes and readjusted his pants before the door to his office opened. He was sure Claire had scheduled more appointments with his members, so he was surprised when he saw his youngest brother walk in instead.

"Bill, quiet." The little dog stopped his howling and laid back down, putting his gray face on his stubby little legs before falling back to sleep.

"Miles, do you know *you* have a dog in your office?" Peirce looked skeptically at the dog. "And is he wearing a bandana?"

"Yes. He's easy to miss being so close to the ground and all, but that long tail is lethal when he wags it. As for the bandana, I had one from when we go riding. It just seems right for him, don't you think?"

"I'm glad I came then. One, you're not a dog person. Two, Morgan's been in town for a week and you've disappeared since then. I know Marshall is who you normally talk to and he's tied up with all the last minute details for the wedding next month, and Cade is all baby talk nowadays. And Cy, well, who knows what he's doing? So, I thought the responsibility fell to me to come check on you."

Miles looked up at his baby brother and almost laughed. Pierce was ten years younger than him and was just a kid when he went off to join the Rangers. He still thought of him that way even though Pierce had just bought his first farm and was in the process of rebuilding the old farmhouse by hand while he cleared the land. Miles and the rest of his brothers had even turned over control of their farming to him for the past five years, but it was hard to think of him as a confident adult.

"Tell Ma I'm fine, just busy."

"You think Ma sent me? I came because I'm the only one who's noticing you're not yourself. What's going on? I'm shocked you've decided to keep this mutt."

"Bill was sitting on my front porch this fall and has just decided to hang around. He's a pretty cool dog. Nothing is going on. I'm just working hard to meet with the farmers to try to get a consensus on blocking this takeover." Miles started to get agitated. Who was Pierce to think he knew anything about this?

"Well, Morgan paid me a visit this morning. She put forth a real good argument for Top Producers. Bigger contracts, more bargaining power, lobbying efforts in Washington to help farmers..."

"What?" Miles shot up in his seat. Oh, this meant war. Morgan went to his own family to try to force the so-called merger!

"Yup. I learned her high points and her weaknesses, but I guess you're too busy to hear what your *little* brother has to say."

Miles softened his face. Pierce seemed to have picked up on his lack of enthusiasm while talking to him about business. Miles looked again and maybe his little brother wasn't so little anymore. He was almost as tall as Miles, same hair and eyes, sharper features though and he was leaner. Miles worked out every day to keep in Ranger shape, but Pierce had muscles from wrestling and branding cows, tossing hay bales, and all the other physically demanding jobs of being a farmer.

"You're right. Sorry. Tell me about Morgan."

"You first. You seem so distant recently and it doesn't look like you're sleeping much."

"Pierce, I'm fine. I never sleep much, you know that." Miles sat back in his chair and suddenly felt very tired.

"I know you don't sleep much since you've come back from overseas. Maybe you need to talk to someone," Pierce said quietly.

"I certainly do not. There were people who came home in body bags—I just can't sleep very well. I count myself lucky."

"Well, if you ever want to talk about it, I'm here for you."

"No offense, but you couldn't handle what I saw or had to do." Miles flashed back briefly to the feeling of his hands around a terrorist's neck the second before he snapped it.

"Miles. I can handle it. But if you don't want to talk about it, then let's hear about Morgan, then and now." Pierce sat down and absently started to scratch Bill's head.

"Fine. If it'll make you leave. She kissed me the night I graduated and it was the kind of kiss that stays with you after all these years. We may have kissed since she came back in town and it may have been even better that it was the first time."

"Oh, so she's using sex against you. How can you fall for that?" Pierce laughed.

"I'd never fall for that," Miles said indignantly.

"Oh no? She's out talking to the farmers and you're here moping about her instead of using it against *her*."

"You may be onto something, Pierce. Turn the tables against her and use sex appeal against her."

"Well, let me know how it goes next week at poker night." Pierce stood up and turned to go.

"Hey, Pierce."

"Yeah?"

"Thanks for the advice." Miles watched as Pierce's face transformed back into a boyish grin.

"You're welcome."

Chapter Nine

Morgan thanked the farmer and watched as he drove off down the bare field in his tractor. Last week she had managed to get some signatures and even turn one of Miles's members, but this week was something entirely different. It didn't matter that in the month she'd been here she had garnered a good number of signatures when this week she had failed to get any.

She tucked the unsigned paper back into her leather satchel and started the long trek back to her car through what would be a sweet corn field come summer. Her four-inch heels sunk nicely into the ground. It took her ten minutes to walk back to her car. She was dirty, cold, and pissed. A Keeneston sheriff cruiser sat directly behind her car. Great. Was she going to be arrested again? It was the one thing missing from her teenage days: Old Sheriff Red watching her like a hawk and bringing her to the jail to scare her straight—most of the time for things she didn't even do. So, what was Red going to arrest her for now?

Morgan put on her best game face and then cringed when she saw her reflection in the car window. Her game face resembled a very nasty scowl. The door to the cruiser opened and a woman in jeans and a black fleece with a gold star embroidered on the chest got out of the car. Was she being punked? Where was Red?

"Expecting someone else?"

"Yeah, where's Red?"

"Arizona. He retired there this year."

"And you're the new sheriff?"

"No, my brother-in-law is sheriff."

"Ah, small town nepotism at its best. How I've missed this place." Morgan rolled her eyes and then realized she might be close to crossing the line. She really didn't want to be arrested for some bogus charge.

"Ha! I knew I'd like you," the woman laughed, resting her hands on her hips.

Morgan just stared at the woman in total confusion. Her red hair was pulled back into a ponytail that bounced as she laughed. She was slightly taller than her own five feet five inches and looked very athletic, except for a slightly rounded belly. She also looked very comfortable with having a gun on her hip.

"So, who are you and what can I do for you?" Morgan asked cautiously.

"I'm Annie Davies. I just wanted to meet you."

"Davies? Which one are you married to? And which one is sheriff?"

"I'm married to Cade. He's a teacher and football coach at the high school. We just had a baby at Christmas, but I had to come meet you. Oh, and Marshall is now the sheriff," Annie told her.

"I can see Marshall being sheriff. But, Cade married to a deputy? Were you like a kindergarten teacher before and then got this job when you married into the family?"

"Me? Kindergarten teacher! Hardly! No, I was an undercover DEA agent before I married into the family. I took a step down in my career, but it's been great."

"You were an undercover DEA agent? You're messing with me right?"

"Nope. I transferred up here two years ago from Miami."

"So, why exactly did you want to meet me?" Morgan asked in amazement.

"I had to meet the other black sheep. When Cy comes home there'll be three of us," Annie smiled.

Morgan couldn't imagine what she was talking about. This woman in front of her was as far from a black sheep as she was from a movie star. And what did Cy have to do with it? If she remembered, he was a quiet and serious boy who liked chess. Not very black-sheepish.

"I see you're confused. See, you're not the only one with a bad reputation. I might have a rather thick file at the DEA. I had a rather large chip on my shoulder having grown up in some bad foster homes."

Oh. Maybe she was more like her than Morgan knew. While she didn't grow up in foster homes, she did have a rough home life. It's something that a person with loving parents just wouldn't understand. "What about Cy? He was nothing but a little chess-playing nerd when I left town."

Annie broke out in laughter again and this time Morgan would've sworn she saw tears rolling down her face. "Last time I saw Cy his hair was in a short buzz cut, he had a scar along his jaw and was built like an action movie star. He was the mystery. He claimed he's a farmer, but since he was never here we're all guessing he's doing something very bad and/or dangerous. Underground MMA fighter is my guess."

"No way!" Morgan laughed. She stopped suddenly, realizing this was the first real conversation she'd had that didn't involve explaining herself or doing her sales pitch. It was certainly the first time she laughed since she got back to Keeneston.

"Well, I'll let you get back to work. I just wanted to introduce myself. Feel free to stop by anytime and chat. From what I've heard you know where the sheriff's office is. I'll be back to work in eight weeks, but I like to drop by a lot to make sure they keep in line." With a wink Annie got back in her cruiser and left Morgan shaking with laughter. Wow! Had she just made her first friend in Keeneston? It had only taken just over thirty years.

Morgan sat down in the back booth at the Blossom Café and ordered a tall glass of sweet tea. After meeting Annie, her day went back down the drain. The other three farmers she met with rejected her outright. One even threatened to shoot her. Then she had to drive the two and half hours back to Keeneston. About the time she hit Elizabethtown, her boss had called her.

Her ears were still ringing from that chewing out. He had told her that her time was limited before he fired her. She had three months, and if she didn't secure this takeover by any means necessary, she would be out of a job. After she had hung up the phone, she had an overwhelming desire to go home. Not to her condo in DC, but to Keeneston. She wanted the warm and comforting food from the café. She wanted to hear the voices of those she grew up with and she wanted to pretend for once she belonged.

"Everything okay, dear?" Miss Daisy asked reluctantly as she put down a plate with a huge slice of red velvet cake, dripping with rich cream cheese frosting.

The red of the cake matched the red hearts the Rose sisters had decorated each table with for Valentine's Day. Just one more thing to make her feel like crap. She wondered if Hallmark made a card for women like her—"Happy Valentine's Day. One more year celebrating your spinsterhood."

"Why would you think it's not? And why would you even care?" Morgan asked as she forked in a large bite of cake.

"Maybe because you have this sorta dazed look in your eyes and you forgot to order dinner. And we do care, we always have."

Morgan just raised an eyebrow in disbelief.

"Okay, maybe that's a stretch. May I recommend the chocolate chess pie for your next course."

"Yum. Sounds perfect." Morgan gave Miss Daisy a hesitant smile and was rewarded when she received one back. It was a slightly awkward moment, but as she watched Miss Daisy walk away she suddenly felt relieved. Something shifted inside her, just like it had when she talked to her mother all those years ago.

"May I join you?"

"Hmm?" Morgan broke from her thoughts and looked up, then up some more into Miles's hazel eyes.

She noticed they were greener tonight. Morgan also remembered that they turned dark brown when she had kissed him. Her eyes traveled to his lips bringing memories of the office kiss flooding back. He had so gotten better with age like rich bourbon aged to perfection. And, man, was he aged to perfection.

"Um, Morgan?"

"Yes?" she asked, still lost in her fantasy.

"You've got something..."

She watched as Miles reached out toward her. She closed her eyes in breathless anticipation. He was going to kiss her again. She just knew it. Her body yearned for his touch. For the feel of his hand caressing her face before bringing his lips to hers in a feverish kiss—the feel of his finger wiping her face with a napkin. Morgan's eyes snapped open in time to see him pull a napkin with a white smudge of frosting on it.

"You had some frosting. So, may I join you for dinner?" Morgan felt her face turn pink and ducked her head hoping Miles wouldn't see it.

"Sure."

"What are you having?" he asked with his deep southern voice. She blushed again thinking about the way his husky voice vibrated through her when he was close to her. The voice, the body, the way he kissed... God, she wanted him. "Morgan? Is everything alright?"

"Oh, yes! Yes!" Morgan clamped a hand over her mouth and looked wide-eyed at Miles. He sat across from her with a huge grin on his face. His five o'clock shadow made him sexier than sin and she knew right then that he knew she hadn't been answering him.

"Well, that's good to know." He reached across the bistro table and covered her hand with his.

He made a slow circle with his thumb that sent heat shooting straight through her... Morgan leapt up, but Miles still had hold of her hand. Her knee hit the table sending it tipping in the opposite direction. Morgan watched as the huge slice of red velvet cake slid right into Miles's lap. Oh God. What was wrong with her?

"If you didn't want me to have dinner with you, you could've just said so," Miles said as he put the plate back on the table.

"Oh dear!" Miss Daisy hurried forward with a towel in hand. "Bless your heart, let me help with that."

Morgan felt her eyes widen as Miss Daisy pulled up a chair, sat down next to Miles, and started wiping frosting and cake off of his lap. It was the first time anyone had seen Miles turn red with embarrassment. He grabbed Miss Daisy's hand as it wandered closer to the center of his lap.

"I think I can take it from here," he said with his blush deepening.

"Are you sure, sugar?" Miss Daisy asked as she scooted her chair back.

"I'm sure, thank you."

Morgan bit her lip to stop from laughing as Miles finished wiping the frosting from his lap. She watched as Miss Daisy smiled and gave him a wink before heading back to the kitchen.

"You know, I think you did that on purpose," Miles teased. "And to make up for your bad behavior you need to go out on a date with me. Morgan, will you be my Valentine?"

Morgan stopped laughing and moved her eyes from his lap to his face. "Are you serious?"

"Of course I am."

"You've hated me for years and now you want to go out with me? And not just on any old day, but on Valentine's Day? That's not reasonable and if you're one thing, it's reasonable," she said suspiciously.

"Morgan, I've never forgotten that kiss and I fully intend to explore those feelings more. I'm very serious about taking you out on a date and I can't think of anyone I'd rather spend Valentine's Day with. It'll be fun to put business aside for a night and just focus on us.

I'll pick you up at seven." Miles's eyes turned brown and his voice turned sensual.

"Okay. I'll see you then," she smiled as she pushed back her worries. He was offering her the one thing she never thought she had and she couldn't resist grabbing the carrot he was dangling. Could her dreams be coming true after all this time?

Miles stood up and wiped some more crumbs from his pants. He gave Morgan a killer smile and walked out of the café. Pierce had given him the idea to turn the tables on Morgan and use his sex appeal against her for a change. It had started off that way, but it had certainly ended differently.

There was no denying he was attracted to her, but he found that it was more than that. He had fun with her. He enjoyed the challenge that she presented, but was amazed by the comfortable feel that enveloped him when they started talking. Sometime during their talk at the cafe, his date idea had turned from a business tactic to something he was really looking forward to. He had avoided Valentine's Day since college. However, he found himself looking forward to it this year. God, he just hoped his mom didn't find out about this or she'd be booking the church. But, the real question was if Morgan was just playing him.

Miles unlocked the gate and drove toward his house. The geese honked their welcome and Bill howled his hello. He turned off his alarm and turned to Bill. The old dog sat down and thumped his tail. His short, stumpy legs caused his belly to get support from the floor.

"Hey, bud" Miles smiled again as Bill sat up, his front feet dancing in the air as he balanced.

Miles tossed him a treat and headed to the living room. He shrugged his wide shoulders out of his suit coat and tossed it on the back of the chair. He poured himself a drink and sat by the large bank of windows as he thought about Morgan. It was just like all those years ago. She was intoxicating. Once he touched her he couldn't get her out of his mind.

Miles drifted off to sleep in his chair with Morgan on his mind. But like most nights, the pleasant dreams were chased away by his darker ones. With no control over his mind it took him to the place he hated most. Back to those mountains.

Afghanistan, six years ago…

Cade was unconscious after being nearly beaten to death. Miles knew he didn't have long before reinforcements showed up. They were supposed to hike into ally territory with their rescue and be picked up in two days' time. He ran to his brother and had to look beyond the swelling and bleeding to find the depth of his injuries.

Cade's nose was broken, most likely one or both of his eye sockets were broken, and he had a huge knot on the side of his head. Miles went to pick up his brother when he finally felt the fire shoot through his body. He felt the pain of the bullet wounds as he tried to drag Cade to the now empty, sporty black Subaru off-road sedan. He stopped and raised his weapon when he heard a noise. He listened closely as he approached the caravan. It was a banging noise and he could hear muffled screaming.

Miles opened the front door to the car and made sure it was empty. He grabbed the keys from the ignition and dragged Cade into the back seat of the car. With his gun in hand, he walked back around to the trunk. He inserted the key and turned it. The trunk popped open and a young blonde woman with wild eyes stared back at him.

Miles's eyes opened as Bill's barking woke him from his nightly purgatory. He thumped his tail and waited for Miles to walk him outside. He looked at his cell phone as he stood out under the stars and waited for Bill. He had fallen asleep at ten o'clock. It was now two in the morning. Four hours was a lot for him. It was so much in fact that he was now wide awake.

He changed his clothes and walked downstairs into the basement gym to work out his frustrations and develop a plan of action. He had a company to defeat and a woman to date.

Chapter Ten

Miles pulled up to the hotel in Lexington and took a deep breath. He'd been on lots of dates, but this one felt different. He made his way through the lobby and knocked on the door. He lost his breath when Morgan opened the door wearing a skintight black dress.

"You look beautiful," he said as his eyes soaked in every curve of her body. Her luscious breasts, her small waist, her rounded hips leading to some very sexy legs. Images of his hands all over her flooded his head. He remembered that he was holding a flower and extended the single red rose to her.

"Thank you. Where are we going?" Morgan asked somewhat shyly as she sniffed the rose.

"I thought we'd go out to dinner at a lovely place I know not too far from here."

Miles held out his arm and felt so proud when she placed her small hand on it. He escorted her out of the hotel and walked the short distance downtown to a restaurant located in one of the historic buildings.

He laughed as she told stories of her time on Capitol Hill and she laughed when he told her about the pranks his siblings liked to play on each other.

She couldn't believe the time he had managed to talk Red into letting Cade go for a prank gone wrong. Miles had told Red, "If you want to arrest my brother for running down Main Street in nothing but what God gave him, then wouldn't you be saying what God created wasn't good enough? Furthermore, I think Edna will shoot you if you keep blocking her view. Shouldn't his punishment simply be to finish the run home with every woman in town watching? Red had buckled as the crowd grew and Cade finished the run in the buff with scores of people following in their cars cheering him on. Miles had failed to tell Red the reason Cade was naked and running down the street: he was chasing Miles and Marshall for sneaking to the pond and stealing his clothes while he skinny-dipped with a girl from college. It was the last prank they had played before they had been deployed.

Dinner was over before they knew it. He felt special to have seen this side of Morgan... the real side. The side that donated time to charity and would stop traffic in front of the White House to chase down a dog wandering in the street. He had laughed as she told how she had slammed on her brakes, jumped out of the car, and held up her hands to stop traffic. The Secret Service came to investigate the disturbance. Soon enough, she had all of them running about trying to catch the smush-nosed pug.

It troubled Miles to see Morgan's warm, caring side and know that he might have been misjudged her all these years. He stopped at her hotel door and waited for her to find her key.

"Thank you, Miles. I had a wonderful time," Morgan said as she pulled her key out of her purse.

"I did too. Best Valentine's Day yet. Do you think we can take a break away from business next Friday and do this again?"

"Is this Friday too soon?" she teased.

"I wish, but I'm being dragged to a tux fitting for Marshall's wedding. It's less than a month away and Mom gave us a bunch of things to do over the weekend. As she says, 'March is only a blink away.' She's on a mission to get everything done early so we're not rushing the week before."

"Sounds nice actually. Good night, Miles, and thank you for such a wonderful night."

Miles stepped closer to her, his body alert with desire. He gently placed his finger under her chin and drew her close to him. Slowly, softly, he bent down and brushed his lips against hers. Miles had never felt such intimacy in one kiss before. It shook him to his core. He pulled away before he lost all control.

"Good night, Morgan."

Miles was lying on his bench press, lifting weights, when he heard his phone ring. He glanced up at the TV's cable box to see that it was only six in the morning. It was never good news when the phone rang that early.

"Davies."

"Miles. Tabby." Miles grinned at Old Man Tabernacle's to-the-point greeting. "I got a problem."

"Have you been arrested again?" Tabby was notorious for trying to write his name in the snow, but was rarely arrested when the temperatures were above freezing.

"No, it's my pigs. They're sick."

"Have you called Katelyn?"

"She just left. She thinks it's poison, but has no proof of it. All my older pigs died, but she thinks the younger ones will make it. She's going to run some tests and ship out some samples." Miles thought he heard a trace of emotion in Old Man Tabby's voice.

"What can I do?"

"I thought it was just suspicious that it happened the day after Morgan came to see me."

"What?" Miles bolted up from the bench.

"She stopped by yesterday and gave the Top Producers pitch. I turned her down flat and then the next morning I woke up to find my pigs poisoned. I wanted to know if you could do something about it."

"I'll talk to Marshall and Katelyn and see what they say. I'll let you know what I find out."

Miles hung up and immediately his phone rang again.

"Hey, Marshall. I just got off the phone with Tabby. What's going on?"

"I don't know. Katelyn's equipment isn't up to testing for most poisons, so she's sent it off. It'll take a week most likely. Do you think Morgan did this?"

"I don't think so, but I'll keep an eye on her."

"Let me know if you find anything out," Marshall told him.

"Will do. See you in a couple days for tux fittings."

Miles lay back down on the bench and lifted the weighted bar above his chest. He concentrated on his breathing as he added more reps, wondering if Morgan was really capable of poisoning. The madness and confusion were driving him to push himself harder. She was a delinquent, but when he kissed her he felt as if she was part of him. Who was the real Morgan Hamilton?

Miles pushed opened the door to Katelyn's veterinary clinic and walked into a packed waiting room. Bill's tail wagged as he walked confidently through the sea of cats and dogs.

"Miles. How ya doing?" Shelly asked from behind the receptionist desk.

"Fine thanks."

"I heard the tux fitting last week went well. My sister-in-law's best friend's second cousin works in alterations and she said that the ladies were fighting over helping y'all. A little tip—you might want to tell the guys not to walk out of the dressing room in only their tux pants. Y'all almost got old Mrs. Scranton trampled by young seamstresses. Oh! And who is this handsome young man?"

"Shelly, meet Bill." Bill sat up and held out his paw to shake. "Katelyn said she got the test results back and I hope she doesn't mind, but Bill's a rescue and I wanted him to be checked out."

"That's fine. Come on, hon, let me take you to an exam room. Katelyn wanted to see you right away to give you the test results."

Miles walked through the lobby and into the exam room with pictures of puppies on the wall. The past week and a half had been quiet. There had been no more incidents of poison or other mischief. Morgan hadn't acted strangely and while people weren't happy to have her driving all over the state trying to persuade them to force the sale of Family Farms, they hadn't complained about any inappropriate behavior on her part. Miles was seeing her again tonight for their second official date, even though he had checked up on her a couple of times since their last date. Especially when he found out Top Producers was doing everything they could to delay the grocery store deal, or at least that's the reason he told himself he was calling her. Deep down he knew it was because he couldn't get her out of her mind. The way they talked, the way they laughed and the way they kissed.

The door opened and Katelyn came in wearing scrubs and a white jacket with her name embroidered on the breast pocket. She smiled at Miles before sitting on the ground to introduce herself to Bill. Bill looked at her with his big round brown eyes, and Miles watched as Katelyn fell under his spell.

"He's adorable! I didn't know you had a dog, Miles."

"Bill's a rescue. He just kinda found me a couple months ago." Miles shrugged his shoulders as he remembered Bill sitting on his porch.

"That's how it usually works. So, I got the tests back from Auburn. Old Tabby's pigs were poisoned with ANTU. Usually they die from hypoxia within 2–4 hours of ingestion. Pigs that survive over 12 hours will most likely recover, which is why the younger ones lived. They had healthier systems to begin with."

"Could this be something they accidently got into?" Miles asked.

"Maybe decades ago when it was used some for rodent control, but not anymore. I've already talked to Tabby and he said he doesn't use it anywhere on his farm. It was definitely a case of intentional poisoning. And, before you ask, I've checked around the area and there have been no other cases of this." Katelyn stroked Bill's head, which he had rested on her leg.

"That's very interesting. I assumed you told Marshall already."

"Yes. He's also brought Noodle in on this. Our wedding is just a couple weeks away and we want someone to know all the details in case something happens while we are on our honeymoon."

"That sounds like a good idea."

"Now, let me see this cutie. My, you're a sweet old man, aren't you?" Katelyn looked at Bill's teeth, "Probably nine years old or so." She finished running her hands over his long body and tested his joints. "He's in great shape. I must commend you for deciding to keep him. Older rescues are the hardest to find homes for. I think you two will be good for each other."

"Thanks Katelyn." Miles patted his leg and Bill jumped up from the ground, "Let's go bud."

Morgan pulled back right in time for another door to slam in her face. David was so not going to like this. She had only managed to secure ten more signatures this week. Any means necessary was what David had told her and it looked like she was going to have to up the ante to defeat Miles.

She didn't want to hurt him. He'd shown her such kindness since she came back to Keeneston. And their date had been so romantic. She loved his dry sense of humor and the way he always seemed to be looking out for her. He would casually guide her through a crowd, hold the door for her, and make sure she was having a good time. Not to mention the way her body caught on fire when he just looked at her. Oh, and when he kissed her! His lips were a gift—that was the only explanation because the way he kissed was enough to turn a saint to a sinner.

Tonight was their second date. She knew she was crossing a line by dating her opposition, but it wasn't like she hadn't crossed the line a couple of times during her life. She couldn't stop touching her lips, remembering the feel of their kiss.

They had both been busy trying to defeat one another in business so they had decided to have dinner at the Blossom Café. She was sure he was doing just as much traveling as she was. When Miles suggested meeting at the café, Morgan actually became more nervous. Everyone in town would know about the date within the next couple of minutes and that would only heighten the gossip being flung about.

Morgan pulled down Main Street and silently laughed at the confused faces debating whether they should wave or not. Apparently her car was similar to a very popular resident, and everyone was taken aback. For the past two weeks people started to automatically wave and then would stop midway to peer into the tinted windows to see if they should continue or turn and run.

Morgan parked her car and headed into the café. Conversation stopped momentarily before the gossip started back up. She looked around and found Miles sitting at his usual table in the back of the room. The closer she walked to him, the quieter the people became. When he stood up, smiled, and helped her into the chair she could have sworn she felt a tidal wave of air as every head turned to look.

"It's good to see you again, Morgan," Miles said as he scooted her seat forward.

"You too. How are all the wedding details coming along?" she asked, trying to think of safe topics.

"Great. Katelyn is going to be a beautiful bride according to my sister. I'm playing the dutiful best man role and have made sure all the groomsmen make it to all the required events and such."

"Just two weeks away. Are you all having a wild bachelor party?"

"No. We're just having our weekly poker night and the girls are getting together too. Now, let's talk about something more interesting." Miles' voice dropped and she felt her heart instantly pick up.

"Morgan! What are you doing here?" the shrill voice of one of her worst nightmares squealed in fake excitement.

"Kandi Chase, as I live and breathe! It's so good to see you." Morgan plastered on her best screw-you-with-a-smile face and looked up into two huge things that weren't there when Kandi was tormenting her in high school. "My goodness! You sure have changed since high school," Morgan said as she pointed to them.

Kandi thrust her chest forward, "I know! Aren't the girls lovely? Men love them, don't they Miles?" Morgan choked when Kandi thrust them toward Miles.

"I'm sure your husband enjoys them. After all, he did buy them for you." And there it was, one of the reasons Morgan had fallen for Miles in high school. The very dry sense of humor he used to cut people down without them even realizing it.

"Why don't you find out for yourself, Bachelor Number One?" Kandi thrust the girls toward his face causing him to lean so far back Morgan thought he'd tip over.

"No thank you. Oh, look, there's your husband now."

Morgan stifled her laughter at the relieved sound of his voice as a balding man with a potbelly walked in and looked around. Morgan watched as Kandi gave a pout with her fully injected lips before she turned to flounce her way to her husband.

"Bachelor Number One?" she asked as Miss Daisy put their order on the table.

"That's right. Miles here is the top bachelor in Keeneston," Miss Daisy told her with a big grin.

"Really? Who else is on this list?"

"Marshall, but he's obviously off the list now. Then there's Henry Rooney, do you remember him?" Morgan saw Miles roll his eyes and lean back in his chair for the inevitable girl talk.

"Henry Rooney…. hmm, black hair?" Morgan asked as she thought back to high school.

"That's right. I gotta ask—what was he like in high school?" a sprite of a young woman from the next table interjected.

"Who are you?" Morgan asked the new woman to the conversation.

"Tammy Fields. I'm Henry's secretary. I just have to know. Anything embarrassing that can be used for blackmail would be preferential." She put her hands under her chin and leaned forward to hear better.

"If my memory is right Henry played basketball and hit on every girl in the school." Morgan smiled as Tammy giggled. She appreciated the woman's pink-tipped blonde hair and friendly face.

"That's him alright. He's still like that."

Morgan looked back to Miss Daisy and found Miles picking at his food. She should feel sorry for him, but she didn't. "Who else is on this list?"

"Ahmed," Tammy sighed and then fanned herself.

"Now, I know I didn't go to high school with anybody by that name."

"He moved here, what five years ago?" Tammy questioned as Miss Daisy nodded in response and then headed off to another table. "And he's *yummy*! There's a sheik here that owns the farm next to the Ashton's. Ahmed is his head of security. Dark, dangerous and damn sexy."

"Oh! I may need to meet him," Morgan laughed as she, much to her surprise, fell easily into girl talk with this young woman.

"Excuse me? I guess I need to remind you that you're on a date with me. I'm number one on that list after all." Miles said dryly.

"Oh my god! You're actually on a *date* date? Not just a business dinner, but a *date*?" Tammy's voice rose and suddenly the café was quiet again as the tidal wave of air hit her when everyone turned at once to look her over again.

"Yes, we are. If you'll excuse us?" Miles politely said goodnight and then turned back to Morgan. "Well, now it's out there. I give it ten minutes."

"Are you kidding? News like this will be all over town in five." Morgan laughed as she took a bite of dinner.

She was having such a good time with him. Every time he looked at her, every time he touched her, she felt her feelings for him growing. It wasn't high school all over again, it was something with a lot more substance that just a high school crush. Which made what she was going to have to do tomorrow all that much worse, but nothing was going to stand in her way of forcing the sale of his company. Even realizing that she still loved him. Damn, why couldn't anything be easy?

Chapter Eleven

Miles ignored the sweat dripping down his face and over his stubble. His legs were burning, but he pushed himself harder. His legs screamed in pain as he forced them to move faster and faster along the grass path. Miles's breathing was slow and controlled as he pushed his body to its limits.

It was five in the morning, another hour and a half until sunrise. The air was cold, but he didn't feel it. He had started running almost two hours ago. Bill had long given up trying to follow him across the pastures and with a sigh had collapsed into a heap on the ground. Forty minutes later as Miles made another lap by the house he saw that Bill had managed to make it onto the patio furniture and was fast asleep on the chair.

Through the still early morning air, the sounds of sirens drew his attention from his running. He slowed down and turned toward the sound behind him. In the distance an orange glow cut through the darkness. It only took a split second for Miles to leap into action. He pushed his legs faster, harder, as he pounded over the frost-tipped grass. He kept his breathing slow and steady as his mind raced. He had to get home and to his cell phone immediately. Marshall would already know. But he needed to call his parents, Pierce, and Cade immediately or they could lose everything as the orange glow overtook the night sky.

As he sprinted to the porch, Bill lifted his gray face off his paws. Instantly the dog was on his feet, his nose in the air. Miles grabbed his phone from the small patio table and called Pierce.

"Dude, this better be good. I had two more hours of sleep before I needed to get up." Pierce mumbled into the phone.

"The Likens's property is on fire! The wind is blowing south and we have cows in that pasture," Miles told his brother as he ran for the barn with Bill right on his heels.

"Crap!" The phone call ended abruptly as he imagined Pierce leaping from bed.

Pierce would know what to do from here. Animals got spooked by fire and smoke, and when a herd of cattle got spooked it was impossible to get them to move in the right direction. If they didn't hurry, those cattle would be too frenzied to move to the far pasture where they'd be safe. They could stampede and then be too out of their minds to watch where they were going. They could get hurt and damage the property.

Miles shoved open the barn door and raced for Mach, his most seasoned horse. He pushed three on his speed dial and soon heard Cade's voice. "I know Miles. Annie just got the call. Justin and I will meet you there." Miles didn't bother saying a thing. He didn't need to. Cade had already hung up.

Bill barked madly from where he had climbed up onto some hay bales. Miles fastened the western saddle on Mach and looked down at what he was wearing—black athletic pants and a tight black Under Armor shirt. He hadn't bothered with a jacket when he had gone running, but now he didn't want to take the time to go inside and get one. Instead he grabbed the black bandana he used when he was mucking stalls and tied it quickly around his face to help with smoke inhalation.

Bill barked again and stood up on his back legs as he danced in circles. "You think you can handle this?" Bill barked again as Miles swung his leg over the saddle. Miles leaned over in the saddle and Bill leapt into his arms. "You need to be still, okay?" Bill sat on the saddle in front of Miles as if he was a Dalmatian on a fire truck while Miles urged Mach into a gallop.

Miles gave Mach his head as the black horse thundered down the lane heading straight for the fire. Bill whined as they approached the pasture. The fire was right across the street. The one fire truck from Keeneston was already in place, trying to prevent the spread of the fire. He was sure Lexington had already been contacted for backup. The Likens family stood watching as the fire ravaged their apple orchard. Miles would talk to them later, but now it was only a matter of time before the cattle broke down the fence.

Through the smoke he saw a dog dart toward him, his long black and white hair flowing behind him. The hot pink bow on his head helped Miles see the bearded collie as the smoke filled the area. If Justin was here, Cade was somewhere in the smoke. Bill barked madly as he waited for Cade to clear the smoke and find him.

An old pickup slid to a stop and he saw his mother climb out. She was still in her pajamas with a big coat thrown on in haste, her blonde hair pulled back into a messy ponytail. She ran toward him in her cowboy boots.

"I have water and bandanas to help you boys breathe. I also have first aid and a couple gallons of water for Justin. I see Bill wants to help." Marcy Davies lifted Bill down from the saddle and placed him on the ground. "There's Cade now. Pierce and your father are right behind me. Here's your whistle—remember all the codes?"

Miles nodded his head as he grabbed the orange whistle and put it around his neck. One blow meant move forward two meant to stop. They also had codes for right, left, straggler, and anything else you could think of.

Cade took his whistle and put it over his cowboy hat. Miles turned when he saw his mother look away and saw Pierce and his father, Jake, galloping toward them. His mother handed out the whistles and bananas as she stood in the center of the group giving orders. "Take them to the back pasture on Marshall's property. It's the farthest away. I'll follow along in the truck if you need anything.

It'll also deter the herd from running into the fences. Form a U along the fence closest to the fire. Jake will take point in the center. Miles, you and Bill take the right flank. Cade, you and Justin take the left. Pierce, you work next to your father and once we get them moving, he'll take the lead and you make sure none are left behind. Now go!"

Miles pulled the reins on Mach and hurried toward the pasture. Bill stayed with him as his short legs ran double time to keep up. His mother opened the gate and let them through. The pasture was eighty-five acres and there were close to one hundred cattle scattered everywhere. Their eyes were large with fear as the smoke hid the fence line and the other cows from each other.

Miles felt the heat from the fire instantly as he raced along the far fence line to get to the right side of the pasture. When he made it to his position he looked down, surprised to see the dog had kept up with him. Bill's long tail was arched over his body, his tongue hanging out of his mouth, and a light was in his eyes that Miles had never seen before. Miles blew his whistle to signal he was in place. He was the last one to get there.

His father gave one short blow to signal the start of the round up. Miles leaned over to Bill, "Okay, let's see what you can do. Go!" Bill shot off, his long tail low to the ground now as he sped off like a bullet. Miles grabbed the rope looped over the horn of his saddle. He carried it in one hand and used the other to steer Mach.

Bill ran fearlessly up to the huge cows and when they didn't listen he would nip them on their hocks. Miles watched in amazement as a thirty-five pound dog forced cows that weighed almost a thousand pounds to do his bidding. Miles and Bill worked in tandem for hours as they cleared the area of cows and pushed them together in the center of the pasture.

Sweat ran down his chest as he yelled at a cow to get moving. His voice was low and scratchy from so much yelling and the smoke he'd inhaled. His eyes stung with smoke as he coughed into the bandana. He heard one of his group signal that they had a stray. Deep barking rang out over the calls of the cows and Miles knew it was Cade. Justin had gone to bring the stray back into the group.

"Miles!"

Miles turned around to see his father galloping toward him, his jacket flapping in the wind. The gray in his hair was hidden under the soot that covered them all. "We're clear in the back. You boys need to close in. We're not too far apart now. I'm going to the lead and find Rocky to lead them out of here."

Miles nodded and knew the old bull would be eager to get the cows and their calves out of the rectangular shaped pasture. The hard part was done, finding all the cows, now it was all about timing and leading. He went to yell a command to Bill, but Bill had heard Justin and was already pushing the cows toward his barks.

"Yeehaw!" Miles yelled as he used the rope to deter a cow from turning back. Through the haze he saw Pierce closing up the back of the herd and his father at the head. Rocky's big horns led the way following his dad toward the gate.

Pierce, Cade, and Miles curved along the back of the herd and waited for them to fall into line as Rocky lumbered forward. Pierce looked the worse for wear of the brothers, having spent the most time closest to the fire.

"How you holding up, Pierce?" Miles shouted.

"Fine. That's one helluva fire. I saw Marshall and Annie working to coordinate the fire trucks from all the surrounding counties and to keep the gawkers at bay," Pierce yelled, wiping some sweat from his face as the morning light brought a new perspective to the situation.

A quick whistle blow from Jake brought the dogs to their feet. Justin led the way, barking to get the cows to move forward in line. His pink bow was now stained black and was close to falling out as he ran from right to left barking at the cows. Bill worked with him to keep the cows in line. As Justin ran to the right, Bill ran to the left. Miles and Cade took their positions about halfway up in line on each side of the herd. It took another forty minutes, but finally they were out of the pasture and a good way down the dirt road leading to Marshall's land.

At the sound of rumbling, Miles turned to see his mom and Katelyn in the pickup truck. "Here you go," Katelyn said as she leaned out the window with a bottle of water. Miles drank from it thirstily and then tossed it in the back of the truck.

"Thanks. I needed that. Maybe you should take Bill with you in the truck."

"It looks like you got yourself a true farmhand," Katelyn replied. "He may be old, but he's in great shape. After the cattle get moved, make sure you give Bill small amounts of water over an hour. He may be sore, but he's not doing anything that will hurt him. He's doing what comes naturally to him. It's amazing to watch him and Justin working this herd."

Miles nodded and then they were off to give his father some water. Once on the road and away from the smoke, the cattle moved at a steady pace to the far pasture. They knew the way since they were rotated between the pastures a couple times a year. The dogs worked to push the herd through the gate. Once the cows were in the pasture they instinctually went forward to the pond to drink.

Miles dismounted and led Mach over to where Katelyn was filling up water buckets for the horses. Bill and Justin were laying side by side in the shade of a large maple tree and Miles would've sworn they were both smiling.

"Those two were unbelievable. We've never moved a herd so fast before." Cade said as he took off his shirt and used it to wipe the sweat and soot from his face.

"Here you two go." Their mother handed them wet bandana to clean themselves.

"Thanks, Ma." Pierce grabbed one and sat down with his brothers. "I wonder what happened. Trees just don't go up like that. Especially when we've had rain recently."

"I'm sure Marshall is already looking into it," Jake said as he took a seat next to his sons. "After this break, let's ride back up and make sure we don't have any damage. Then we'll get cleaned up. Your Mother said she has a big dinner for us."

Miles looked up at the sky. The early afternoon sun was shining and Claire was undoubtedly wondering where he was. He'd get home, shower, and get some work in before dinner. The Likens were part of Family Farms, so he'd make sure to check on them. Hopefully it was only the front part of their orchard and they had saved the other three fields. It would still be a huge hit to them, though.

"But if you'd only listen to me Mr. Johnson. The offer is up to twenty-three million dollars. You'd still own your farm, you'd just become part of the Top Producers family. You'd have their power and their brand behind you."

"Look little lady. I don't know nuttin' about Top Producers, but I've known Miles Davies since he was knee high to a cricket and I trust him with my life and my family's. I also know about you. I remember that time you and your little criminal friends went cow tipping on my property. It was only because of your father, God rest his soul, that I didn't call Ol' Red on you and have you tossed in jail." Mr. Johnson tugged up his jeans and took a step forward, pushing her out of the doorway and onto the small wooden porch. "And if you don't get off my land right now, I'll call Sheriff Davies and have you arrested for trespassin'."

"Mr. Johnson, I'm sorry for my past childish behavior. I'm not that person anymore."

"Bless your soul, I hope not. Now, get!" Mr. Johnson slammed the door and Morgan was left, for the second day in a row, with a door slammed in her face. Yesterday evening Mr. Likens had done the same thing.

Morgan looked at her cell phone and saw a missed call from David Washington. It was seven in the morning and her boss was already calling to check on her. And, what did she have to report?

Nuttin'. Yesterday she'd spent the day in southern Kentucky. She hit up farmers in Corbin, London, and Somerset. She'd come back to Keeneston and got rejected, rather rudely if she may say so, from Mr. Likens and his son. David had called her on his way home from work and she'd delivered the bad news. Out of the eight farmers she'd visited, only one had agreed to the merger and two previous signees had called her to tell her they had changed their minds and decided they were sticking with Family Farms.

"Hi David, it's Morgan."

"Did you get the Johnson farm this morning?" David asked, cutting to the chase.

Morgan slumped her shoulders, "No, sir. He's an old family friend of Miles and refuses to agree, no matter the price."

"I hate these small town imbeciles. So stuck into their old ways. We'll just have to do more to shake them out of it. Time to get tough, Morgan. No more asking. It's time to force their hand." David disconnected and Morgan was left wondering what other ways she could try to force their hands.

"I'm too tired for this," Morgan mumbled to herself as she drove back to her hotel. She hadn't slept much recently and this new "get tough" initiative called for more than she was willing to do so early in the morning. Last night with the Likens was tiring enough and now all she wanted was to go back to the hotel, take a shower, crawl into bed, order room service, and watch a movie. She'd tackle the remaining list starting tomorrow.

Chapter Twelve

Miles slipped on his dress shirt and had just started to button it when he heard the doorbell ring. He jogged down the stairs as he tossed his tie around his neck. Looking out the window he saw Mr. Likens's Dodge Ram. Miles had actually been planning on going over to see how he was doing after he finished getting dressed.

Miles disarmed the alarm and unlocked the door, "Mr. Likens, how are you? I was just on my way to see you."

"You're a good boy. Thank you. I was actually coming to check on you. I'm sorry I didn't come yesterday, but we were tied up all day with the police and then the insurance adjustor. I saw you all herding the cattle yesterday morning during the fire. I hope none of them were injured," the older farmer said. His blue jeans were covered in mud from all the water the firemen used to put out the fire. His gray hair looked disheveled and Miles was relieved to see his son standing a few steps behind him. Farming tended to be family business and as Mr. Likens got older, his son had taken a more active role.

"Hi Garrard."

The younger man nodded his hello. Garrard was about ten years older than Miles and had been a great neighbor so far. He, his wife, and teenage daughters were regular visitors to his parents' farms.

"The cattle are fine. We didn't have any property damage. Come on in." Miles held the door open and waited for the Likenses to come in. "How is your orchard?"

"Luckily it only took out half of the front field. Garrard was milking the cows when he smelled the smoke. He and the farmhands were able to get hoses on it pretty quickly to prevent it from spreading further. They were able to slow it down long enough for the Keeneston Fire Department to arrive."

"Do they know what caused it?" Miles asked as he sat down across from the men.

"It was arson. They found an empty gas can nearby," Garrard told him as he shook his head.

"Who would do such a thing?" Miles asked more to himself than to the Likenses.

"I don't know, but I do know that Morgan Hamilton was the last person we saw before the fire," Garrard said not too convincingly. It was clear by the way he said her name that he thought she was responsible.

"And you think Morgan did this?"

"I know you went on a date with her and all, but what you don't know is that I saw her last night when she came to our farm. She started talking to Dad about selling and Mom called me to come over. When I arrived, she and Dad were arguing. I told her under no uncertain terms that we were going to agree to a merger when it was really nothing but a fancy word for a takeover. Dad told her we'd been friends and business partners in one way or another with your family for fifty years. We weren't going to agree period and then he slammed the door in her face."

"I'm not making any judgments, Garrard. I promise to look into everything and everyone. My top priority isn't my love life—it's the farms and families of those members in Family Farms."

"I know it is, son. We just thought you should know all the facts. We also wanted to make sure everyone was alright. Tell your father and mother we'll see them at the wedding if not sooner."

"If I know my mother, she'll be over soon with some food."

"That's the best thing to come out of this. Shoot, it might be worth it to burn the orchard ourselves to get some of her peach cobbler," Mr. Likens joked as he and his son walked out the front door. "Now take care of you and yours. If you need anything we're just a shout away."

"Thank you."

Miles shut the door and leaned against it. Could Morgan really have done this? She allegedly poisoned all the mums for homecoming junior year. Could that have escalated to arson? The ringing of his phone stopped his contemplation.

"Hello, this is Miles."

"Miles, Jim Brannon down in Somerset."

"Good morning, Jim. What can I do for you?" Miles and Jim were cut from the same cloth. Jim had served in the Army during Vietnam and had the same warped sense of humor one could only have from seeing the things they had both seen during active duty. They used that humor to deal with those memories. There had been an instant camaraderie when they met for the first time.

"I'm having some trouble out here on the farm I thought I should tell you about." Miles felt his stomach harden—not another fire. "Around one o'clock this morning someone tried to kill my sheep."

"What do you mean, tried?"

"Molly, my border collie chased them off. But not before they dropped something, a container of ANTU. I haven't seen that stuff in years."

"I know the stuff. A man up here in Keeneston had his pigs poisoned with it. Let me ask you a question. Did you have any visitors recently?"

"Yes," Jim said knowingly. "It's the reason for the call. A lovely lady from Top Producers came by the other day. She wasn't taking no for an answer about agreeing to the merger. I had to threaten her with a shotgun to get her off the property. I have her card here—Morgan Hamilton."

"I'll take care of it, Jim. You have my word." Miles was already grabbing his keys. He would put a stop to this right now. Morgan was going to answer for what she had done.

"I knew you would. And don't worry about us. There's no way Brannon Farms will be agreeing to any merger—regardless of their underhanded tactics."

"Thanks for the support Jim. I'll keep you updated." Miles disconnected and strode toward his car.

His anger rose with each step he took. Morgan had played him like a fool. She had distracted him with dates and niceties. She had drawn him in, just like she had that night she kissed him at the graduation party. She'd done a hell of a job keeping his attention on her. He couldn't decide who he was angrier at—her for these crimes or himself for developing feelings for her.

Miles pressed on the gas and sped toward Morgan's hotel. He wouldn't allow her to distract him again. He wanted answers and he was going to get them. If there was one thing Miles really knew how to do it was interrogate. As the calmness that accompanied his anger spread over him, his mind took him back to his last interrogation.

Afghanistan, six years ago…

The cave was dark. The only light came from a small bulb powered by a generator. "We captured him crossing over from Pakistan. We know he's part of the terror cell that has made numerous threats against the West, but he's not talking. We did find a picture on him though," Lieutenant Pike informed him.

"Of who?" Miles asked as he looked back into the cave at the man handcuffed to a chair in one of the military's secret safe houses along the border.

"Mariah Brown, the Secretary of State's daughter. She's near the Afghanistan and Tajikistan border with her school on an archeological dig." Lieutenant Pike handed him a picture of a pretty blonde-haired girl smiling into the camera.

"Okay. I'll see what I can do." Miles tapped the photo against his camouflaged cargo pants and headed toward the man. Miles slowed his heart rate and breathing. He banked any and all of the emotions he felt as he approached the man. His deadened eyes reflected his dark thoughts. He had found that if terrorists saw any emotion they'd try to play on it. However, if they thought you didn't care if you died along with them, they'd tell you anything you wanted to know.

"I want to know everything you know about this picture," Miles said calmly as he turned the picture for the bearded man to see.

"Why should I tell you anything?" he asked in English accompanied by a heavy accent.

"Because, my government does not recognize that I'm here. I can do whatever I want to you and no one will ever know. Let me be clear on one thing. Look into my eyes as I tell you this." Miles paused and waited for the man to look him squarely in the eyes. "I will kill you if you don't cooperate and it won't be quick. Do you believe me?" The man's eyes went wide and he slowly nodded. "Good. Now tell me everything you know about this woman."

Miles walked back out of the cave and handed the picture back to Lieutenant Pike. He took a deep breath and blinked to bring himself back from the dark place he went for the job.

"There's a caravan tomorrow. She'll be there. Cade," Miles said loud enough for his brother to hear and to come over to join them. "Cade and I will go secure her. You take him to the base in Afghanistan. Just drop him off gift wrapped at the gate. Our presence here is classified, so I don't want you talking to anyone. Go dressed in local attire. You know the routine."

"Yes, Sir." Lieutenant Pike saluted before stepping into a side cavern to change clothes along with another member of the Delta Force.

"You scare the hell out of me when you do that dead eye thing and you're my brother," Cade tried to joke as they saddled up their horses. The area was so rocky that horses were the best means of travel. They could also avoid checkpoints easier by cutting through the mountains than taking the local roads.

"I scare myself too," Miles whispered as he slipped on a long white Kameez shirt over his uniform and wrapped the patterned scarf around his head. "Let's go rescue this girl."

Miles bounded up the stairs to Morgan's floor. When he found her door he took a deep breath. He banked his emotions, hardened his eyes and swore to himself that he'd make her pay for what she had done to his friends.

He knocked calmly against the door and waited. Nothing. He knocked again, this time a little harder. Nothing. Miles pressed his ear to the door and heard a voice. She was definitely in there, but was just refusing to answer the door.

Miles pulled out the small leather case from his inside coat pocket. He was going old school to get this door open. Pulling out his pick he inserted it into the manager's override lock and in short order heard the sound of the lock releasing. He put away the picks and opened the door to Morgan's room.

The first thing he saw was the towel on the floor. The second thing he saw was Morgan's back to him. Her black hair was wet and skimmed her naked shoulder blades as she slid into a pair of dark purple lace panties that sat low on her hips. A small black tattoo of a horse was low on her back and drew his eye instantly. She wiggled her hips and broke out in song. It was then he saw the small white buds in her ears as she danced around.

Miles leaned against the door and crossed his arms over his chest to enjoy the show. Morgan put her arms up and shook her shoulders as she sang and danced to the music. She was probably cleaning up from being chased across Jim's field by his dog. And here she was, singing and dancing as if nothing happened.

Morgan turned as she danced and dropped her phone when she saw him. The white ear buds were yanked from her ears as she leapt away from him. "Miles?" she asked from across the room.

She sure did sound nervous. Good. She should be. He slowly uncoiled himself and stepped out from the shadows. He ignored the fact that she was mostly naked, but was surprised when she didn't bother to cover up her gorgeous breasts.

"Let me guess, you just finished washing off the evidence from your early morning trip to Somerset. Did you stash your muddy boots with your smoke-ridden clothes from the fire you set yesterday morning?" Miles took a menacing step toward her. He raised an eyebrow slightly when Morgan didn't back away. In fact, she crossed her arms, thrusting her bare breasts out, and stepped toward *him*.

"I don't know what you're talking about, but you sure as hell shouldn't have broken into my room. You could've called if you wanted to ask me something," Morgan said sternly.

"Sure! And the infamous Morgan Hamilton would've told the truth. Look at me, Morgan," he waited until she looked him in the eyes. "I will have the truth from you. Tell me everything about your sabotage of my members' farms." That should do it. Miles waited for her to crumble to the ground spilling all her secrets.

"Infamous? You little prick! I've never lied to you. I told you it was me that painted that tower. You could've shown everyone the note, but *you* chose not to!" She pointed her finger at him and took another step forward. Her violet eyes flared bright as her skin turned red with anger. Why wasn't she crying yet? "And really, sabotage? You think I would sabotage your farmers? To what end? How would that help me?"

"I know you did it to Jim Brannon, Garrard Likens, and Mr. Tabernacle. Oh, you think you're so smart using an older poison like ANTU. Did you really think we wouldn't notice that Jim's sheep *and* Tabby's pigs were killed with the same poison? Where is it? Hand it over *NOW*."

"You think I poisoned sheep and pigs? Are you delusional? I don't even know what the hell ANTU is! You come in here and accuse me of this without even asking – *you're* a pig! And if I did have any of that ANTU stuff I'd poison *you* with it, not some helpless cute pig!" she yelled at him while waving her arms about.

Miles looked around the room then. He looked for muddy boots, dirty clothes, or evidence of ANTU – anything to use against her. The clothes that were on the floor of the bathroom were clean. Her shoes lined up in the closet were all clean and none were proper for running about farms.

"Don't turn away from me! I'm not done with you yet! How dare you break into my room! What did you do, bribe your way in from some cute cleaning lady?"

"No, I used to be a Ranger. I just picked the lock." Miles almost smiled when her eyes went large. Here came the fear and crying. He narrowed his eyes again. Phew, he was beginning to think he was losing his touch.

"Oh." Why didn't she look afraid? Instead she looked like she was contemplating something. "That explains it perfectly. However, I'm still really mad at you and you should apologize right now for breaking in and accusing me of such horrid things," she said pointing her finger at his chest.

He gave up. He had tried his best interrogation looks, voices, and body language and she hadn't trembled once. In fact she had just handed it back to him tenfold. "Explains what?" Miles questioned as he took another step toward her. Well, there was more than one way to string a bow and he'd just use a more delicate method.

"You were always looking out for the little guys – protecting them. You made sure the chess team didn't get their heads swirlied in the toilet by the football team, and you didn't let people pick on me when you were in earshot. You, Miles, are a classic protector. It's one of the reasons I fell in love with you in high school. I never had anyone try to protect me before. But, I have to tell you – you're way off base here. I'd never hurt anyone or anything and you should've trusted me when I told you that."

Miles looked at her again. She was right in front of him and this time he did notice that her breasts were just inches from his chest. As their anger faded he could tell by her uneven breathing that she had just realized it too. Miles reached out and caressed her arm. He let his hand fall to her waist as he pulled her against him.

Her breasts were even fuller than they had been in high school. It was a heady feeling having her body against his. He leaned forward and gently traced her ear with his lips.

"What... what are you doing?" she asked on a shaky breath.

Miles trailed his lips down and gently nibbled the side of her neck, using his tongue to lave the slight pain away. She moaned and leaned closer to him. She rolled her head to one side, giving him free access to her neck.

"Did you poison the pigs or burn down the orchard?" he murmured against her neck before kissing it again.

"No," she said on a moan.

"Do you still love me?" he asked before moving to place another succulent kiss on her neck.

"Yes," Morgan answered so quietly he barely heard it. She tried to pull away then and cover herself with her hands.

"Don't you dare," his gravelly voice reprimanded. "You're beautiful. Never cover up around me." He pulled her back against him and let her feel his hardness against her stomach. Miles moved his lips to her mouth and stroked her tongue with his, leaving her breathless.

Through the haze of passion Morgan felt his hand glide up her ribs and stop slightly under her breasts. He was so close. She had to have his hands on her. She was throbbing with need as he touched her body. Finally, with strong hands, he cupped her breasts and gently rolled her nipple between his fingers.

"Let's finish what we started all those years ago." Morgan hardly recognized her own voice as she pushed Miles down on the bed and straddled him.

Morgan ripped off his shirt and sent buttons flying in every direction. She was emboldened when Miles just smiled, urging her on. She ran her hands over his ripped abs and writhed along the length of his arousal. Miles ran his hands up her thighs and she melted.

"Nice panties. Now take them off," he rumbled.

She heard the tearing of lace and saw her panties fly through the air. His hands took their place. Her head rolled back in pleasure and all conscious thoughts fled.

Chapter Thirteen

Morgan snuggled against Miles's chest and drank in his scent. The real thing had been so much better than her fantasies. As she ran her hand over his chest she noticed the puckered scar on his arm, a long straight scar across his ribs and another circular scar on his side. Was this from being a Ranger? Had he actually been in battle?

"Miles, why did you believe me when I told you I hadn't done the things you were accusing me of?" She absently ran her fingertip over the long white scar on his chest.

"I have the ability to determine when someone is lying or not under certain circumstances. I knew you were telling the truth when I asked you that final time so I moved on to more… um… important things." He grinned and ran his hand through her tumbled hair.

"How can you do that?"

"The Rangers taught me a few tricks."

"I think we just did some of those tricks," Morgan teased. She reached over his chest and put her finger on the long jagged scar. "How did you get these scars?" Morgan was hoping that the subject would keep him away from remembering that she had told him she loved him during the heat of the moment. Although he didn't acknowledge her answer, he knew enough to ask her.

"There was a rescue mission and I was injured."

Morgan felt her eyes widen. There was so much she didn't know. She had started a new life that seemed so small compared to what he had done with his. "Who were you rescuing?"

"At that exact moment, my brother Cade. He had been captured by terrorists. This scar I got trying to get him and another rescued hostage to safety. I was shot. Then I was cut with a knife—a dirty one for that matter. The tetanus shot hurt more than anything, I think," Miles tried to joke.

She could tell that whatever happened may have been a while ago, but was nowhere near forgotten. "Miles…" Morgan stopped when she heard his phone ring. It was probably for the best. She was about to blurt out that she had loved him in high school and now she wanted to be the one to love him forever. She also wanted to be the one to take care of him.

"Hello? What!" Miles sat up in bed so fast that Morgan rolled off his arm and onto the pillow. Whatever that was about, it couldn't be good. "I'll be there in a couple minutes." Miles jumped out of bed and stepped into his black boxer briefs without even giving her a second thought.

"Miles, what's going on? Is everything alright?" Morgan pulled the covers up as she watched him zip up his slacks.

"Where were you this morning?"

Morgan's back went stiff with his accusatory tone. "I think you know where I was this morning or you wouldn't be asking. Now, will you stop being a jackass and tell me what is going on?"

"One of Mr. Johnson's cows was killed. I'm heading over there now."

"Wait just a minute. You don't think I did this, do you?" Miles didn't answer and she watched as he continued to get dressed. "Miles. Wait, I'm coming with you." She went for her boardroom voice to hide the hurt she felt. They had just made love and now he was turning a cold shoulder to her.

Morgan sat quietly in the passenger seat of his car as they drove down the dirt lane toward the back of Mr. Johnson's farm. In the distance she could see the flashing police lights. From the corner of her eye, she could tell that Miles was watching for her reaction. It hurt her more than all the teasing she had received during high school.

A cow lay on the ground on the other side of the fence. A blonde-haired woman was kneeling in the grass beside it. Her long hair was pulled back into a ponytail and she had a stethoscope hanging around her neck. Marshall Davies was standing behind her in his uniform. He certainly hadn't changed much since the last time she had seen him. He just got thicker and his face had matured, losing its youthful mischievousness.

Miles was already walking toward his brother when Morgan opened her door and got out of the car.

"What's going on?" Miles asked.

Marshall put his hands on his hips and looked back at Morgan. "A cow has been shot. It's dead."

Miles nodded and didn't seem to notice that Marshall had said that to her and not to him.

"Hello Morgan. It's been a while. I'm glad you're here. I have some questions for you."

Morgan crossed her arms over her chest and stood perfectly straight. "I'm sure you do," she said coldly. Some things never change. She felt as if she was seventeen again, standing in front of Red and being blamed for something her angelic sister did but blamed on her.

"Where were you this morning?" Marshall asked as he stared her down. She felt sorry for the teenagers of Keeneston. Marshall was a far worse fate to deal with than Red.

"I was here from 6:45 to a couple minutes past 7:00 this morning. Then I went directly back to my hotel." Morgan looked him in the eyes and returned the stare. She may feel seventeen again, but she wasn't and she refused to be intimidated anymore.

"Katelyn, dear," Marshall turned to the woman veterinarian. Oh, so this was the woman he was marrying. Morgan had been hearing about the wedding since she got back to town last month.

Morgan watched as the woman stood up gracefully and walked over to them. She was tall, and by her posturing she was mad and thought Morgan was at fault. Katelyn stood almost six inches above her and was staring Morgan down, trying to intimidate her.

"How long has the cow been dead?" Marshall asked.

"Two hours at the most," Katelyn answered.

"Morgan, can anyone verify you were at the hotel two hours ago?" Marshall had pulled a pad of paper out and Morgan just waited. Would Mr. Rangerman be compelled by the truth to step forward and tell his brother what he was doing two hours ago?

"I can."

Marshall turned to his brother and raised an eyebrow. "I was with her from seven-thirty till now at her hotel." Miles finally slouched a little and let out a breath, "And she didn't commit the other crimes either."

Marshall looked between them. "How do you know?" he asked his brother.

"She passed the test."

Marshall just nodded and wrote something down in his notebook. Katelyn was obviously confused and wanted clarification. "What does that mean?" she asked Marshall.

"It means you didn't do it. Any of it. The person responsible is still out there. Morgan, do you have any idea who did do this?"

"No."

Miles looked over at Morgan and knew in an instant that she was lying. No one could tell unless they were trained, but her pulse jumped and she forgot to breathe for a split second. She didn't do it, but did she know who did? Was she covering for Top Producers? There was a lot more to this story and he was going to get to the bottom of it.

Katelyn thanked Miss Lily for the glass of Rose sister special iced tea and leaned back in her chair. She had just told the story to the girls at her bachelorette party at Wyatt Estate. Miss Lily and her grandmother, Ruth Wyatt, had planned the event. All the Rose sisters, her best friend and matron of honor, Paige, were there along with Kenna, Dani, and her soon-to-be sister-in-law, Annie.

"So, she didn't do it?" Dani asked in confusion as she took another sip of water.

"Miles said he asked her and she passed the test. Marshall just accepted that, but he didn't have time to tell me what that meant."

"That doesn't sound like the only test she passed," Annie joked as she gave the crowd a wink and took another bite of cupcake.

"Eww. That's my brother. I don't even like thinking about how you got pregnant with Cade," Paige said as she made a face. "What it means is that Miles is basically a human lie detector. It's uncanny. He can detect changes in your breathing and eye movement. He can even feel when you lie."

"I think he was feeling a lot more than a lie," Annie sputtered. "Sorry! Sorry! I can't help it. Miles does nothing remotely interesting and yet he's doing the horizontal mambo with the bad seed of Keeneston? I mean, look at how petrified you all are!"

"It wasn't that she was just a bad seed, but bless her heart, she was the spawn of Satan. She was constantly at the center of everything bad that happened. Even her own father and sister turned their backs on her," Miss Violet told them as she brought in more cupcakes.

"The last time I saw her she was tearing apart my rose bushes. I had to chase her away with my broom before she destroyed them for no reason!" Miss Lily clucked.

"I'm sorry, but I disagree with you all," Annie jumped in. "I've talked to her and I really like her. She may have been that way when she was seventeen, but she's not like that now."

Kenna bit her lip and furrowed her brow. "So, if she didn't do it, then who did?"

"I don't know, but I think I need more chocolate if we're playing detective," Dani said as she picked up another cupcake. "I also think it's Katelyn's bachelorette party and we have a duty to get her wasted."

"Here! Here!" Kenna toasted. "To Katelyn and Marshall!"

Miles swirled his bourbon in the crystal glass and watched as the amber liquid circled around. It was doubtful that the glass of bourbon held the answers he sought, but the warmth that overtook him as he drank it sure did help. Morgan was lying to him and he wanted to know why.

Miles looked up as his brothers and friends took their seats around his poker table and collected their chips. Mo had joined them tonight, along with Ahmed, Dinky, and Noodle to make their normal poker party considerably larger. However, tonight was Marshall's bachelor party and not the brothers' weekly poker night.

"I'm not lucky in love nor at cards, so I can just deal if y'all would like," Dinky, one of Marshall's deputies, said as he took a seat at the extended table.

"That'd be great. We usually have to wait for Pierce to lose his money before we get a dealer," Marshall joked as he took the seat next to Miles. "Hey man, thanks for hosting this shindig tonight."

"Of course. It's my pleasure." Miles took another sip of his bourbon and pasted on the fake smile that he had perfected since his return from overseas.

"I'm sorry, but your regular poker night for a bachelor party is lame," Pierce whined as he opened his beer. "Where's the strippers? Where's the music and party?"

"Poor Pierce. You still haven't learned about women at all, have you?" Cade teased his brother-in-law and Mo gave a chuckle.

"What does that mean?" Pierce puffed up his chest defensively.

"I wouldn't mind knowing either," Dinky said as he leaned forward, not missing a thing.

"It means boys dream of strippers, men dream of their women waiting for them at home," Mo said while he shrugged out of his Armani suit coat.

"It also means that once you reach a point in your relationship that you're getting married, you don't care about those things anymore," Cole told his youngest brother-in-law as Pierce just rolled his eyes.

"In my case it means that I'd be shot if I came home wearing glitter." Cade joked about his gun-toting wife, getting a smile out of Ahmed.

"I don't think I'll ever feel that way about a woman. I'm enjoying my freedom, thank you very much," Pierce said as he picked up his cards. "However, when Miles gets married I'm calling dibs on hosting the bachelor party."

"Speaking of Miles getting married, how's Morgan?" Marshall asked with a grin as the men at the table laughed.

"There's nothing going on with us." Miles took another sip of his bourbon and hoped that would put an end to the discussion, but he knew better. It had only begun.

"Yea, nothin' going on when you were at her hotel for two hours the other morning," Noodle snickered.

"Thanks for keeping that quiet, Marshall. I didn't tell them about Ruffles attacking you when you climbed into Katelyn's window that one night. Death by poodle, very manly. I don't know how you made it out alive," Miles shot back.

"Hey, I had to put it in the police report. You were her, um, *alibi,*" Marshall laughed.

"You know, I think Morgan is perfect for you. You need some excitement. She'll be just like my Dani and keep you on your toes."

Mo tossed another chip on the table and Cole cursed, folding his hand.

"She's very attractive. But, why is everyone so scared of her? I've run a background check and the only thing remotely interesting is the horse tattoo she has on her lower back," Ahmed said casually as he raised his boss's bet.

"How do you know about that?" Miles almost leapt across the table at the thought of someone else seeing Morgan's body.

Ahmed just smiled and Miles took a deep breath. They were teasing him. It's what guys did. So instead of putting his fist through Ahmed's face, Miles just smiled and put his cards on the table.

"I believe the pot is mine." Miles grinned and raked in his winnings.

As the players started to drop out, they talked about Noodle's girlfriend who had asked him to accompany her to the Doctor's Ball. Mo gave him advice on small talk and Pierce mumbled something about them not having strippers either.

"How is you new house coming, Pierce?" Cole asked after he lost another hand.

"It's coming along. The property is run down. I'm in the process of demolishing the house. Selling off the fixtures and whatnots to some of the antique stores. As soon as that is torn down, I can start building the new house. I've only cleared about 8 acres so far for farmland. It's so overgrown that it's taking forever to get ready for crops. Hopefully next year it'll be in condition for me to move in and start planting."

"Maybe you can have your twenty-seventh birthday party out there. Strippers and all," Miles stated dryly. "All teasing aside, we're proud of you little bro."

"Aw! You're growing up!" Cade grabbed him and ran his knuckles over Pierce's head as he squirmed. "What are you laughing at, Mo?" Cade let go of his brother and Miles watched as Mo's grin widened.

"I'm simply imagining if I did that to one of my brothers at the palace. My father would be horrified."

"How are your royal duties going?" Marshall asked as he tossed a chip in the center of the table. Mo was so down to earth most of the time they all forgot he was a prince.

Mo played with a chip and looked at his hand before tossing out his chips. "My father is in grand preparations for when he gets his heir at the end of the summer. He wants to send me around the world to represent the family at conferences. He believes that with me living in the United States it shows other countries, especially English speaking countries, that Rahmi is the better choice to do business with than some other countries in the Middle East. As an expectant father, he thinks they'll find me less intimidating now."

"That's rough. Will Dani go with you?" Cole asked as he sat back from the table after losing his last chip.

"Some. She'll go to New York City with me when I speak to the United Nations, but from there she'll come home and I'll be on my way to Belgium to meet with the European Union. I don't want her traveling too much in her condition. She's not quite ten weeks so I want to keep everything as stress-free and normal as possible."

"It's very exciting. I'd love to see all those places. I wonder what kind of fishing you do in Belgium?" Noodle pondered.

"It sounds exciting, but it's not. You don't have time to see what that fishing would be like. Every minute is scheduled. All you see is the airport, the inside of a car as it drives through the city, and then the hotel. You don't do much else but shake hands with politicians and try to figure out what everyone is after."

"Sounds like a game of Clue," Dinky said to Noodle who just nodded. Miles even smiled at that.

Mo just shook his head and raked in his winnings. "I fear it's getting late," he said as he and Ahmed pushed back from the table. "It's been a pleasure. Congratulations Marshall. Katelyn is a wonderful woman and I wish you both all the happiness in the world." Mo shook Marshall's hand and gracefully slid his suit coat

back on. At least Miles wasn't the only one there in a suit.
"Goodnight everyone." Mo waved and Ahmed gave a nod to them before heading out the front door.

"It's time I headed out too." Noodle rose and shook Miles's hand as he thanked him. "Good luck at the weddin' boss. Just one more week to go."

"It'll be here before you know it." Dinky clasped Marshall on his back as he got up to leave too.

"As much as I hate to admit it, I need to go too. I need to get up to put hay out for the cattle tomorrow, which you all should be thanking me for, by the way, since most of them are technically yours." Pierce slapped his dark brown cowboy hat against his jeaned-clad leg as he got ready to leave.

"Aw, you're so cute. We thank you by paying you—nicely at that—for managing our farms." Cade ruffled Pierce's hair as if he was a little boy.

"You've done a good job with our farms. I hope you won't leave us when you start your own farm." Marshall gave him a hug and walked toward the door.

"Nah. I wouldn't leave you all like that. Congratulations. Katelyn is a great girl. Just remember, I get to plan Miles's bachelor party—it's not like Cy will be back anytime soon to usurp him as the next brother to fall." All the brothers nodded in agreement and then looked at Miles with smiles full of mischief.

Miles tossed the last of the uneaten food in the trashcan and held it open for Cade to toss the empty beer cans. Everyone had gone home except Cade who had offered to stay and help clean up.

Miles still couldn't believe Cade was a new father. He seemed so calm and secure in his new role. How had he let go of everything that happened to him during the war? He envied Cade and Marshall for that. To feel that kind of love, to feel safe and secure in life again—it was a fairy tale for him.

"Miles, there's something I think we need to talk about." Miles grew worried when Cade talked into the trashcan instead of looking at him. "We need to talk about you. I can tell you're not sleeping. Is it nightmares?"

"It's nothing. I assure you, I'm fine," Miles said stiffly and even he cringed at the harsh tone in his voice.

"It's not fine. You've been pushing yourself for too long. You need to get professional help—or at least talk to me about it. You haven't talked to anyone about the war. I don't even know what happened to me after I got knocked unconscious that day. You've never told me. All I remember is the beginning of a fierce beating and the feel of a gun being pressed to my head. The next thing I knew I woke up at Ramstein Air Force Base in the hospital."

"You won't be able to understand what it was like. I don't *want* you to know what it was like. You won't be able to handle it. No one can handle it," Miles trailed off.

"I can, trust me. I can handle it. Talk to me Miles. Or I can give you the name of the professional I saw when I got back home." Cade took out a business card and placed it on the table next to Miles.

"You went and saw someone?"

"Yes. You know what I went through. I was waking up with nightmares of the feel of the gun to my head. I'd jump at sounds. I started to isolate myself and then I started to drink—heavily. I was afraid I had post-traumatic stress disorder. So I went and talked to someone who helped me cope. They helped me relearn how to function outside of a war zone."

Miles looked at his brother with new eyes. No, no one could understand the horrendous things he went through with his brother and young Mariah Brown. He learned that he had a dark side—a dark side that could kill with no feeling. And why should he go whining to a therapist when so many other soldiers didn't make it out alive? Miles shook his head. He was just an ungrateful bastard. No therapist needed to tell him that.

"Look, just think about it." Cade waited until Miles nodded before he continued. "There's something else. Annie and I have been talking and we want you to be Sophie's godfather. Would you do that for us?"

Miles was shocked. It wasn't that he disliked babies, but most people thought him too serious to take care of a child. "Me? Are you sure?"

"Yes, you. You protected me with your life. I know you'd do the same for my child."

"I'd be honored to," Miles said sincerely.

"Then I'll let you get some sleep. Annie will be thrilled to know you said yes. Good night, Miles."

Miles watched his brother climb into his Highlander and drive off. A godfather. He could do that. Deep down he loved babies. He took care of all his siblings after all. At the thought of babies, he ignored the pull at his heart. Miles knew he'd never have one of his own. No one would want to marry someone with so much dangerous baggage attached. So, it was up to him to be the best godfather possible.

Chapter Fourteen

Morgan stepped off the plane with her carry-on and walked through the crowded terminal at the Ronald Reagan International Airport. She glanced at her watch. If everything went as planned she'd meet with David and be on the red-eye back to Lexington within hours. No one in Kentucky would even know she was gone.

After the incidents at the farms she had visited she knew more drastic measures were needed. Morgan had called her boss and David had instantly asked if anything eventful had been going on. She knew he had already heard the news about what had happened to the farmers. Morgan told him she wanted to talk to him about it in person and David had insisted she fly out immediately.

Morgan looked around and saw the black stretch limousine with her name on it. She allowed the driver to open the door as she slid into its luxury. Morgan looked out the window as they passed the national monuments and headed for the Capitol Hill district. David's office was in an old townhouse on the edge of the Hill in a residential neighborhood.

The old townhouse came into sight sooner than Morgan would've liked. She had been trying to think of her plan, but instead found herself thinking of Miles. Would he ever be able to understand what she had done… even if it was inadvertently?

David Washington was waiting at the front door for her. He was slightly older than Miles, forty-two years compared to thirty-six. Unlike Miles he was a short and squatty man who lived on the power he had gained over the years. His light brown hair was thinning and his round face was highlighted by his square black-framed reading glasses.

"Welcome back home, Miss Hamilton. We're the last ones left so I want to lock up if you don't mind. We don't want any interruptions." David reached around her and flipped the deadbolt on the door. "Let's go to my office."

Morgan followed David through the reception room and up the creaking staircase to the offices upstairs. She passed her office and looked at the closed door. She'd only been away for a month and yet it felt like forever. They walked down the Persian carpet runner to the large office suite in the back of the building.

David held the door open and Morgan walked through. A couch and matching accent chairs sat to the far left of the room with a shining wood table between them. Stacks of paper were piled on David's desk that sat slightly in front of large windows reaching almost to the ceiling.

"So, you said it's been eventful in Podunk. What's happening?"

"I think we both know what's been happening." Morgan smiled sweetly and cocked her head. She looked David in the eye and ran her tongue over her bottom lip, "And I think it's working."

"What has been working? Are you trying a new tactic?" David asked with a blank face.

"Not me, but you. I think scaring those farmers is a good start, but they need a final push to agree to sign with me. I'm getting a feel for the town and how they are reacting to your latest efforts. I can let you know if it's worked and give you some ideas of my own next week." Morgan crossed her legs and sat back in the chair.

"I never said I did anything, Miss Hamilton. After all, I've been here in DC for the past month." David mimicked her positioning in his chair and looked at her with one raised eyebrow.

"Oh, I know it's a wink-wink type thing. I just thought I'd offer my help to make it more profitable to us. I think some of the scare tactics could use some tweaking, that's all." Morgan waited for David to respond, but he didn't. He laced his fingers together and rested his pointer fingers against his lips as he thought. There was no sense in pushing it. "Well, I'll let you think about my proposition. While I'm here, I'm going to grab some things from my office. If I hurry I can be back in Kentucky tonight if you don't need anything else." Morgan stood up and slung her purse strap over her shoulder.

"Thank you, Miss Hamilton. We'll be in touch." Morgan nodded and flashed a smile before turning on her heel and walking out of the office. "Oh, and Miss Hamilton. We really need those farms and your clock is ticking," David called after her.

"I'll do whatever it takes to get them for you," Morgan said earnestly before walking out the door.

Miles finished cleaning the kitchen and stared at the business card Cade had left. He picked it up for a closer look. The doctor specialized in PTSD treatment. He opened a drawer and tossed it in. He had way more important things to worry about than spilling his guts to a shrink.

"Come on boy, let's get to bed." Bill wagged his tail, his short legs rushing to keep up with Miles as they checked the locks and armed the security control.

Miles stripped off his clothes and pulled down the sheets on his bed. His legs slid around the soft cotton as he pulled the sheets up to his bare chest. For the first time in his life Miles thought his bed seemed lonely. A picture of Morgan's black hair, fanned out over his white sheets, sent a shot of pleasure through his gut. Could something so wrong be so right?

Afghanistan, six years ago…

Miles felt his heart beating rapidly as he pushed a bloody, battered, and unconscious Cade into the car. He grabbed the keys and slowly walked around to the trunk. The pounding slowed and he envisioned the person in the trunk straining to hear if anyone was coming. Miles took a deep breath and felt the tug of the bullet wound. He took a couple more calming breaths and felt centered. He raised his gun and got ready to open the trunk. He heard every click as he slowly slid the key into place. He opened the trunk and jumped back. Geese honked as they spilled out of the trunk and ran off into the desert.

His eyes shot open. Something had made his geese very upset. His hand automatically reached behind the headboard and pulled out the handgun he kept there. He slid out of bed and pulled on a pair of black athletic shorts. "Bill, come here boy." Bill quietly growled as he trotted over to him. "I need you to stay in the bathroom, okay? Be quiet. No barking." Bill reluctantly laid down on the bathmat and put his head on his paws.

Miles's bare feet padded over the hardwood toward the staircase. With the gun in his hand he quickly looked around the corner and down the stairs. Faint noises came from the kitchen as he quickly and silently came down the stairs. Instead of getting to the kitchen from the living room, he cut through the dining room. A figure in black was leaving the kitchen and making his way to the living room. Miles tossed a look around and saw that the power had been cut. No lights flashed on the oven and the motion detecting lights were off in the backyard. No wonder the alarm didn't go off. He bet the phone lines were similarly cut.

Miles felt the darkness from inside overtake him. His mind and breathing slowed. The heavy gun became part of him. A quick glance showed that the intruder was alone and armed. Miles evaluated the exit points and devised his strategy for attack in seconds.

Miles crept back through the dining room and waited. He knew his breathing was soundless as he tuned into each noise the intruder made. Miles heard him make his way through the living room and to the base of the stairs. He heard the man look up toward the bedrooms and place his foot on the bottom stair. That's when Miles made his move.

Miles lunged from the shadows and took the man down to the hard floor. He wrapped one of his arms around the man's midsection. He used the other arm to reach for the man's weapon. Miles exhaled as the man's elbow connected with his gut. They rolled toward the front door and crashed into it. The gun went flying from his hand as the man timed another elbow to the midsection at the same time Miles hit the door. He didn't feel the pain shooting across his back though. He didn't have time to even recognize the hit.

Miles scrambled to his knees as the man lunged for the gun on the floor. With a growl, Miles launched himself on top of the man. He delivered a series of swift hits to the man's midsection with his knees. The man grunted and tried to roll away from the attack.

The man bounced to his feet and kicked out hard and fast right at Miles's face. Miles grabbed the man's foot and with a sharp twist heard the ankle break. The man shrieked and fell to the ground in pain. Miles was on him in seconds. He straddled the man with one fist full of the attacker's shirt. He held his fist up in the air, poised to slam into the man's face.

"What are you doing in my house?" Miles growled.

"Robbing you, what does it look like to you?" he sneered.

Miles unleashed his hand and smashed it into the man's face. He howled and tried to cover his broken nose. "I'll ask you again, what are you doing in my house?"

"Okay! Okay!" the man took a breath, "I was sent to rough you up a bit." Miles gave a wicked grin in the dark and the man shuddered. "She didn't tell me you were Captain America."

"Who didn't tell you? Who ordered this?"

The man took a deep breath and then looked Miles in the eye, "Morgan Hamilton."

Miles bounded up the stairs to Morgan's hotel once again. Marshall and Noodle had shown up soon after and dragged the intruder away. Miles hadn't told Marshall what the man had told him. No, he wanted Morgan all to himself. He would get every last bit of information out of her before he handed her over to the police.

Miles's long stride ate up the hallway and he approached her door. Not caring that it was three in the morning he lifted his fist to the door and pounded. The door shook under his attack, but didn't open. He was about to pull out his credit card again when he heard the ding of the elevator. Miles looked down the hall and saw a tired Morgan step off with a carry-on bag rolling behind her.

"Where the hell have you been?" Miles roared. Morgan's head shot up in surprise.

"What are you doing here in the middle of the night?" she countered. Miles noticed she failed to answer the question.

"You're under the delusion that you have the right to ask me such a thing." Morgan's head snapped back as if she'd been slapped. "You'll keep your mouth shut and tell me exactly what I want to know or I'll call the police and have you arrested immediately." Miles advanced on her and ripped the carry-on out of her hand.

"If you wanted me arrested I would be already so drop the attitude. What do you want Miles? I'm tired and if you don't mind hurrying this up, I'd like to get to bed." Morgan reached into her purse and pulled out her key card.

"Fine, I have one question for you. Is there a reason you sent someone to break into my house and try to beat me up?" Miles ground out between his clinched teeth.

"What the hell are you talking about?" Morgan snapped back.

"You heard me. I had a nice conversation with the man who tried to attack me and do you know what he told me?" He watched as Morgan simply raised her eyebrow. "He told me you hired him to do so. Imagine my surprise. Here I had thought the sex had been pretty good. If you wanted to break up, you could've just not called me the next day."

"Oh shut up Miles. You don't have to be such a smartass. I didn't send anyone to kill you. You know how I feel about you and it's so absurd to think I'd do that. I don't even know how to respond. So, I'll just say this—if you think I'd do something like this, then you're not the man I fell in love with." Morgan opened her door and then slammed it in his face. Miles looked at the closed door in stunned silence. If this woman wasn't trying to kill him, he might just have to marry her.

Morgan locked the door and hurried to the desk in her hotel room. She plugged in her laptop and pulled out her car keys. On it was a silver horse. She pulled at the saddle and the horse separated, revealing a flash drive. As she inserted the device into her laptop she wondered if she should feel guilty for what she was about to do.

She pulled up the documents she had stolen and reviewed them. She flipped from page to page and reviewed all the data and notes as quickly as possible. She had to find out if she was right or not. If not, she envisioned herself a jailhouse victim of a random act of violence. She didn't kid herself. If she didn't find what she was looking for she might have to grab her bag and run for her life.

Morgan continued to review the documents. It only took a couple of minutes to find what she was looking for. She let out a breath she didn't know she was holding and started to shake. She had found a way to stay alive. Morgan copied the documents onto a new flash drive and picked up her phone. She dialed the number she knew by heart and waited for him to answer.

"I know how to bring them to their knees." She waited for his response and then nodded. "By the end of the week it'll be done. Just hold up your end of the bargain."

Morgan hung up her phone and stripped out of her suit. She climbed into bed, hugged the pillow to her chest and cried. She cried for the loss of a love she'd never have, for the pain of Miles's words, and for the fact that she was just crying. She hadn't cried since her mother passed away, but it seemed a constant struggle against the pain of her past in Keeneston. The tears finally stopped flowing, her nose stopped running, and she finally fell asleep.

Chapter Fifteen

Morgan woke up as the sun filled the room with light. She moaned and rolled over to look at the clock. It wasn't even seven in the morning yet. She wished she had gotten more than three hours of sleep, but there was nothing she could do about it. She needed to get to town and hear the local gossip.

Morgan rolled out of bed and scrubbed the sleep from her face in the shower. There was no better place than the Blossom Café to find out if she'd been discovered. It was sort of like stepping into the lion's den, but the rewards could be just as great. And they had pecan pancakes.

An hour later Morgan pushed open the front door to the café. The noise hit her at the same time as the smell of eggs, bacon, and sausage. As customary, everyone turned to see who was joining them for breakfast. The talking stopped so suddenly that the only noise Morgan heard was the sizzling of bacon.

Morgan tried to smile, but all eyes were narrowed on her and she decided that they believed she had betrayed them. She held her head up high and headed to the empty table in the middle of the room. Slowly the whispers started and soon there was so much gossip flying around that she was afraid she'd be hit in the face with it.

"Did you hear about Glenn Myers's farm? His hay barn was burned down last night. They caught it before it spread, thank God,"

Morgan heard Miss Daisy tell Tammy as she handed her a to-go coffee.

"Oh my gosh! I hadn't heard. Morgan, did you hear that?" Tammy turned and looked at Morgan and Morgan cringed. The café went quiet again except for the sound of chairs scraping the floor as the patrons turned to look at her.

"No. I hadn't heard about that. I'm so sorry for him and his family," Morgan announced to the room instead of just to Tammy who had come to stand next to her table.

"Everyone has been donating bales of hay to him all morning. I don't have any just laying around," Tammy laughed, "but I was going to head over to the feed store and buy one for him. Well, I'll see you later. Toodles!" Tammy gave a little wave and bounced out the door.

"I'm going over there too after breakfast."

Morgan looked at the seat across from her and saw her sister standing there.

"I could pick one up for you if you want," Pam said.

"Thank you, Pam. I would." Morgan reached into her wallet and handed Pam some money. The patrons took notice and started talking again. Apparently she was still suspected, but the gossipers couldn't decide for sure if she was responsible for these criminal acts.

Morgan looked at her older sister and sighed. Pam wasn't going back to her table. "Would you care to join me for breakfast?"

"Thank you." Pam sat perfectly straight in the chair and smiled. Just as quickly her head shot up as the bell over the door chimed. "Oh! My husband is here earlier than I thought. He had to go get the truck to transport the hay." Pam stood up abruptly, suddenly looking nervous. Morgan turned to find a handsome middle-aged man with dark brown hair. He was average height, average build, and had a warm smile on his face. He was perfect for Perfect Pam.

"He looks very nice Pam. Why doesn't he join us for breakfast?" Morgan asked as she scooted over to make room for the brother-in-law she'd never met.

"Oh, um. No. Not today. Sorry Morgan, I just love my husband too much to introduce him to you. I can't take that chance again." Pam hurried from the room.

"What do you want for breakfast?" Miss Daisy snapped. Morgan bit her lip to stop from crying. No one wanted her here. It was time to leave.

"I'm suddenly not hungry anymore. Sorry to have taken a table." Morgan stood up and hurried out the door as the gossip in the café rose to near deafening.

Morgan made it to her car before the tears started falling. Why did she think things would change after all these years? She picked up her phone and dialed. This would end soon.

"Hi," she said into the phone. "Friday at four at the Wal-Mart in Lexington." Morgan hung up the phone and felt a sense of relief. It would all be over soon.

Miles took a seat in the hard chair across from Marshall's desk in the sheriff's office. He had just delivered several bales of hay to Glenn's farm to make sure his livestock was well fed for the next month. The fire the other day had completely destroyed the hay he saved up to feed his animals over the winter. While spring was right around the corner, so was rain and new grass.

"I take it you have news and it isn't some last minute detail for the wedding tomorrow night." Marshall said as he pulled out a pen to take notes.

"Morgan went out of town the other night. She got back around three in the morning. What time did Glenn's fire start?" Miles held his breath. He didn't want to believe it, but Morgan was leaving him no choice. He had tried to see her a couple of times this week, but she had always managed to avoid him. So, he was left with no choice but to turn to his brother to help him find out if she ordered the attack on him.

"Five. I had Annie check with the airlines this morning. Morgan went to DC that afternoon. But, do you know what is even more interesting?" Marshall picked up a piece of paper and tossed it across his desk. "She wasn't the only employee of Top Producers to fly back to Lexington on the red-eye."

"What?" Miles picked up the paper and looked at a picture of a man who had armed forces written all over him. "Who is this?"

"William Brady. His employment record says he's head of security for Top Producers. Do you think he came here to rein Morgan in, do her bidding, or to set her up?"

"That's the million dollar question, isn't it?" Marshall sighed.

Miles had hoped that all the signs were wrong. He knew, while Morgan may not have been the one to actually get the dirt on her hands, the evidence pointed to her having a hand in it.

"Let's go pick her up and have a chat with her. Do you want to come?" Marshall asked as he stood up and strapped on his gun belt.

"Yes. I have to find out if she's involved." Miles was glad Marshall didn't say anything more. His mind and heart were already in turmoil.

Morgan pulled her Mercedes into the busy Wal-Mart parking lot in Lexington. She looked at the clock on the dashboard and slouched back into her seat. She was early and the best thing to do was to stay as still and low as possible. She didn't want to draw anyone's attention during this whole exchange.

She looked around one more time hoping to see the black sedan she was expecting. As she waited, she couldn't stop her mind from conjuring up Miles's image. Their dates had been fun. Morgan still smiled at the jokes Miles had told. She couldn't remember having that much fun. She never had had a reason to smile before. Morgan had been too busy trying to survive high school. Then she'd been too busy working to keep her scholarship and earning money to survive. It should've gotten better after landing this job. She guessed she could finally breathe, but she hadn't. Instead she had worked hard and climbed the corporate ladder.

Morgan hadn't even realized what she was missing until she saw Miles again. Feelings reared up that she had managed to shove down since the night she left Keeneston. However, this time she didn't want to ignore those feelings. The morning spent in Miles's arms had been incredible. She got flushed just thinking about it now. But, there was so much more to their relationship that just hot sex. He made her laugh, he made her look at her life and want to make it better. He gave her hope, he gave her happiness, and she loved him for it. Could he love her though, even after all she had done and all she was mixed-up in now? Especially since he thought she was trying to have him killed.

Marshall held out a pair of binoculars to Miles. He took them and brought Morgan into focus. They had seen her leaving a local farm earlier. Before they could stop her, she had driven off. They had decided to follow her instead. They parked on the far side of the Wal-Mart parking lot and waited.

"Look. Here comes someone. Is it Brady?" Miles said more to himself than to his brother. He trained his binoculars on the black sedan that pulled to a stop next to Morgan's parked car. Morgan got out and leaned over the window. She pulled something small out of her pocket and handed it through the window.

"No. I don't think it's Brady. Is that a flash drive?" Marshall asked.

"I think so. Does she look upset to you?" Miles watched as Morgan shook her head strongly from side to side. It was clear that she and the person in the car were disagreeing about something. Morgan slammed her hand on the car door and then stood still listening to the person in the car. She finally nodded and got back into her car.

"We better stop her now and see what this is about. I don't have much jurisdiction, but I can call in the Lexington Police Department if we need to arrest her." Marshall pressed on the gas and drove as fast as he could toward Morgan. The black sedan already pulled out and was speeding away by the time Marshall cursed his way through the traffic in the parking lot.

Miles decided to let Marshall take the lead on this. Not only was he the law, but Miles was way too close to Morgan to be objective. Miles managed a quick smirk—she hadn't given in to him when he questioned her. He loved it. It sparked his curiosity and his respect when she stood up to him. Marshall slid the cruiser to a stop behind Morgan's car, blocking her in. Miles watched as Morgan got out of her car and stormed toward them.

Morgan slammed the door to the car. The bastard! He was changing the terms of their agreement. She had gotten him everything he had asked for and then said he was changing his mind. That he wanted more. The kicker, if she didn't get it to him he'd leave her out to hang by herself.

She took a deep breath and turned on the car. She had a lot of work to do if she was going to get him what he wanted. She put the car in gear and looked into her review mirror. Miles's angry face filled it. What was he doing here? Could there be any worse timing?

Morgan pulled herself up and stalked toward Miles and his brother Marshall. "Are you all *following* me? How dare you!"

She watched as Miles simply crossed his arms, narrowed his eyes and leaned against his brother's car. Marshall stepped forward with a grim look on his face and she looked back and forth between them. Miles had clearly given Marshall the lead. Not surprising after all of his failed attempts at talking to her this week.

"I have a couple of questions for you."

"Of course you do! But, you don't have any jurisdiction, do you?" she asked smugly.

"What was on the flash drive?"

"I don't know what you're talking about." Morgan crossed her arms over her chest and smiled.

"Who was in the car?" Marshall asked calmly.

"Oh, just now?" Morgan asked serenely.

"Yes, just now," Marshall clipped.

"Just someone asking for directions."

"Dammit Morgan!" Miles roared. He pushed himself away from the car and walked toward her. "This isn't a game. What is going on? Tell us now."

"I'll do no such thing! You have no right to know. You've already decided I've done these things." She turned to Marshall. "You have any evidence to arrest me with?" Marshall simply raised an eyebrow. "I didn't think so. Now, if you gentlemen will excuse me."

Morgan stomped back to her car and thanked God when the car in front of her pulled out. She put her car in drive and left Marshall and Miles standing next to their car.

She stopped at a light took a deep breath. She knew exactly what needed to be done and what was being done to her. She was about to get screwed, and not in the good way. She turned her car toward the interstate and started the nine-hour trip to DC.

Morgan arrived in DC early in the morning. She went straight to the office and parked in the small lot in the back. She glanced around trying to see into the shadows that the yellow streetlights cast around the area. She kept her keys out and walked purposefully toward the back door. She unlocked the door. The sound of the lock tumbling echoed across the lot.

Once inside, she disarmed the alarm and quickly hurried up the stairs. She passed her office and headed straight to David's. She paused then, listening for any sound coming from the other side of the door. When she heard none, she opened the door and headed straight for his computer.

His office seemed eerily quiet as she started his computer. She looked around again when the light of the screen cast shadows around. She was worried she'd be seen and would have to explain herself. While the computer booted up, she went to the massive filing cabinet. Her fingers flew through the folders until she found what she was looking for. She pulled it out and brought it with her over to the computer.

"Crap," she whispered. It was login protected. She tried his name and then the name of his wife. Wrong. She tried his birthday, anniversary, and street address. Nothing. "Think Morgan."

She tapped her fingers on the desk and stared at the blinking arrow next to the password. What was David most proud of? His baby, that's what! Morgan remembered when he bought her. A shiny new Lexus LS sedan. He had showed all his junior partners. He had told them that if they worked hard they too would be able to afford the eighty thousand dollar car that he lovingly called Alexa.

Morgan typed the name in and hit enter. The computer screen came to life and Morgan smiled. She searched through his files until she found what she was looking for. Morgan scanned the information on the screen. What she had here would save her life. She took out her keys and found her silver horse charm. Pulling on the saddle she exposed the flash drive.

Her heart was pounding as she plugged it into the computer's USB drive. She copied the documents to the flash drive. She powered down the computer and stepped around the desk when she saw the light coming from under the office door. Oh God, she was caught!

She stood frozen by the filing cabinet as she watched in horror as the door slowly opened. If they caught her with the flash drive there was no doubt what would happen to her. She'd disappear and no one would be the wiser.

"Morgan? Is that you?" David asked when he poked his head in through the door.

"Oh David!" she sighed in relief. "You scared me to death!" Morgan laughed as she relaxed some.

"I can say the same to you. I was sound asleep when the alarm company called me to say that an expired code was used to get into the building. What are you doing here?"

"Miles is kicking my ass. I wanted to copy his file and see what I could find out. If I couldn't find anything tonight, I was hoping to convince you to have one of your in-depth reviews made," Morgan explained as she held up the thick file.

"In the middle of the night?" David asked as his brow wrinkled.

"Time is of the essence. Miles won't be working this weekend—his brother is getting married. That gives me a leg up. If I can find something on him to force his hand, I can have this wrapped up by Monday."

"I hear you hid the bad news with the good. I must be honest, I'm not too happy with the fact that Miles is doing so well. I was hoping this whole thing would've been wrapped up weeks ago," David said seriously.

"I know. I'm just as upset. These people are loyal to a fault."

"Have you reviewed the file yet?"

Morgan shook her head. In fact, she had a copy of it in her hotel room. She always made copies of his master file. "I got about halfway through it so far. I was just going to make a copy of it now."

"No. You know I don't allow copies of these files."

"You're right. I'll go in my office and take notes of the pertinent items. Is there an in-depth personal review in the file along with my business report?"

"Yes. It's already been done. It didn't show too much. Our evaluation was that the best way to hurt him is to go after what is he holds close to him—his business, the farm, his family."

Morgan was thankful for the darkness or David may have seen her face pale. "I'll get right on this. I think I'll be here for a while. Do you want me to set the alarm when I leave?"

"Yes. Your old code will work for now. I'll give you the new one once you're back in town. Give me a call on Monday and let me know what's happening. I don't want to send Tad to take your place, but you know I'll fire you and give him the job if you can't get it done soon." David waited for Morgan to acknowledge him before he turned and held the door open for her.

Morgan walked past him and to her office. She laid the file down on her desk before heading to the window and looking out. David had parked on the street and was heading toward Alexa with his cell phone to his ear. Who was he calling in the middle of the night? She ducked behind the curtain when David turned around and looked at the office. The streetlight shone on his features and she knew her time was up. His face was set in a glare. His hand grasped his phone with such anger. He knew. She put her hand on her keys and the one thing that would save her.

Chapter Sixteen

Miles stood in front of the bathroom mirror and pulled his black bow tie tight. Katelyn and Marshall may be a low-key couple, but Mrs. Wyatt, Katelyn's grandmother, wasn't. It was to be a black-tie affair tonight. He and the rest of the groomsmen were to be in tuxes and the women were in red floor-length bridesmaid gowns.

As he slid his muscled arms into the tuxedo jacket he heard his phone ring. The number came up as blocked and he instantly knew who it was.

"Long time no hear, Cy."

"Hey Miles. I hear today is a big day. I tried Marshall's cell, but he never picked up," Cy said into the phone.

"He's next door getting dressed. Do you want to talk to him?"

"In a minute. How are things going with you?" Cy asked him.

Images of Morgan, naked and riding him flashed through his mind and went straight to his groin. "Okay. I take it you won't be making it to the wedding. Where are you?" Miles asked even though he knew the answer.

"You of all people should know the answer to that," Cy chuckled. "No, I can't make it. I just left Russia and now I'm going someplace warm."

"Have fun, don't get burned," Miles said dryly.

"I really appreciate you not telling everyone what I'm doing. You're a good big brother and I owe you. If you need something, I'll be there for you. You know that, right?" Cy asked sounding as concerned as Cy ever got—which wasn't much.

"Let me guess, you've been talking to Cade," Miles groaned.

"Don't know what you're talking about," Cy laughed again. "Tell me about Morgan. Is she as hot as she was in high school?"

Miles couldn't explain it, but jealousy shot through him at the thought of his brother thinking of Morgan. "I didn't know you knew her in high school."

"I didn't. I was in middle school, but that didn't mean I didn't look and appreciate. She had some curves you could lose yourself in for days," Cy said wistfully.

"Don't talk about her like that!" Miles ground out before he could stop himself.

Cy responded by laughing harder. "I'll be damned, the mighty oak has finally been felled. Cade and I weren't sure, but now I am. I can't wait to tell the rest of them. Hurry, put Marshall on the phone!"

"Bite me. Remember, I'm not the only one with a secret and Mom will be way more upset if I tell her what you've been up to," Miles threatened. It didn't work. His brother just laughed louder.

"Oh my God. You don't just like her, you're in *love* with her! I bet that's a huge conflict of interest for you. I always saw you with a serious yet pleasant blonde librarian, but you fell for a lawbreaker turned corporate ball-buster. Oh, this is classic!"

"Cy…" Miles warned.

"Okay, okay. I won't say anything. But Cade said there was some problem with Morgan. What's actually going on?"

Miles sighed. Well, if he was going to confide in anyone, it might as well be Cy. Most likely he wasn't even on the same continent, so he couldn't cause too much trouble. "I went and fell in love with her."

"She must be great in bed."

"Cy!"

"Sorry," he laughed, not sounding very sorry at all. "I had to. So, what's the problem?" he asked more seriously this time.

"There's a chance that she's forcing a takeover of my company through intimidation and criminal activity. Oh, and that she may have hired a thug to try to beat me up." Miles sighed and ran his hand through is hair. Saying it out loud made it sound even more ridiculous. How could he let himself fall in love with someone like her? A Keeneston Belle would be a better wife for him.

"What just happened? I heard you curse?" Cy broke his thoughts.

"Nothing."

"Yeah, right. I'm guessing you just thought about the M word. It's only normal when you're at a wedding to think about marriage to the woman you love. I think it's great. Morgan sounds like my kind of woman. Easy big brother—I just meant that I always pictured you with someone uptight and society-oriented. Like a Belle, any Belle. I'm excited you fell in love with the opposite."

"You think it's a good idea that I'm in love with a delinquent and possibly a felon?" Miles groaned, he should've just gone with the flow and started dating Jasmine, the current president of the Keeneston Belles.

"Do you actually think she did everything she's being accused of?" Cy asked.

"Yes. No. Well, I don't think she did them herself, but I think she either knew or now knows who did."

"Ah! That's the crux of your dilemma. If she didn't do it and does the right thing by turning in the people who did or if she had no idea who's behind it, then what would you do?"

Miles was quiet as the image of him and Morgan laughing together crossed his mind. "I'd tell her I love her and beg her to forgive me for acting like such a jackass."

"If you want my advice, I'd stop being a jackass and start working to find out what you're missing and then marry the girl. Now that I have fixed one brother's problem, let me talk to Marshall and remind him not to do that nervous laugh thing during his toast to the bride."

"Thanks Cy. If I can ever return the favor, let me know. I hope you can make it home soon." Miles walked down the hall and handed the phone to Marshall. He couldn't believe he'd been such an idiot. There was obviously more going on than she was sharing. If he hadn't accused her, she might have trusted him enough to tell him the truth. Miles suddenly felt panic welling up. He needed to talk to her. To tell her he knew she wouldn't do these things.

"Okay brother, let's get me married," Marshall grinned as he walked into the room. Miles didn't have time to do it now, but the second the reception was over he'd go find her and get to the bottom of this.

Morgan pressed the gas pedal down and felt her car respond immediately. She took the turn at sixty miles per hour and hoped she'd get there in time. The instant she had seen David turn to the window while on his phone she knew her time was up. She hoped she'd played the whole thing well enough to give her time to get back to Keeneston and talk to Miles.

She had to tell him she had unwillingly put his life in danger. It was time to tell him the truth. Morgan hit the horn and swerved around a horse van. She cut off the large truck as a pick-up truck came toward her in the opposite lane. Morgan took a deep breath as she continued to berate herself. If there was anyone in the world she could trust with her life it was Miles. Instead of trusting him, she'd put him in danger.

The Wyatt Estate's garden was lit with white lights surrounding the front of the historic house. Red roses in large standing vases lined a path around the side of the house leading to the reception site.

Morgan parked her car and looked down at her black suit. The decorations around the house hinted she was going to be grossly underdressed. Morgan was already crashing the wedding, she didn't want to stick out while doing so. She popped open her trunk where she had thrown in some clothes that were meant for the cleaners. She dug through the suits and day dresses until she found what she was looking for: the black dress with a sweetheart neckline that hugged her bust before cascading down to the ground.

She hid behind her car and stripped off her suit and slid into the dress. She took a deep breath and then coughed. Oh God, the dress smelled like an old martini and the trunk of the car. She'd meant to take this dress to the cleaner two months ago. Morgan cursed—she was starting to think fate was laughing at her.

She dug around in her purse and found the small tester bottle of perfume she bought the last time she was at the mall. She sprayed herself in a cloud of perfume and tied her hair into a loose bun at the nape of her neck before hurrying toward the path around the house.

"You sure clean up nice for a delinquent."

Morgan almost slid on the stone path as she turned around to face the deep voice. Pierce sauntered toward her from the parking area.

"Gee thanks. It's so nice to be judged on who you were as a teenager. What were you like as a teenager?" Morgan didn't remember. Pierce was just a little kid when she graduated from high school, but she guessed very few people weren't slightly self-conscious from something during their teen years.

"Look, I'm sorry. But, I can't let you into the reception," Pierce said nicely, but sternly as he stepped in to block her way.

"I don't care what you say, I'm going in." Morgan tried to push past Pierce. He was the total opposite of Miles. He was tall and had the same hazel eyes, but he was so laid back. He always looked like he knew something you didn't and was laughing about it, whereas Miles was always so serious.

"Morgan," Pierce suddenly didn't sound so laid back. He sounded just like Miles. "This is my brother's wedding. I refuse to let you inside and have you disrupt their special night."

Morgan looked up and Pierce was no longer the young man she had seen just a minute ago. He now looked like a man, a very tall, very handsome, very strong man. "Look, Pierce, I have to. Miles's safety is at stake because of me. I have to warn him."

"Why do you care? From what I've heard you only seem to care about yourself and your own entertainment."

Morgan felt the verbal slap to the face and recoiled. "Because I love him! I always have. I need to talk to him."

Pierce rubbed his chin and looked at her closely. She almost squirmed under his review. "Why should I believe someone with your reputation?"

"What part of it?" She felt her voice start to rise, "The part where I graduated high school with honors and earned a scholarship to college? The part where I worked my way through school and into a high-powered job?" Morgan said through clenched teeth.

"No," Pierce said calmly, not reacting to her rising temper in the slightest, "the part where you caused the breakup of my brother and his girlfriend. The part where you almost got expelled from said high school when you put blue dye in the cheerleaders' shampoo and turned them all into Cheer Smurfs. Or, how about the part where your family disowned you?" Pierce leveled his gaze at her and she crumbled.

Morgan felt the tears rise as she bit her lip to keep from crying. She never told anyone about that night. She assumed, incorrectly, that people would forgive and forget. She should've known better. In a small town no one ever forgot anything—even people like Pierce who was just a kid when she was a teenager.

"Look, I'm sorry. Please don't cry." Pierce stepped forward and handed her a handkerchief.

"I don't know if you'll believe me, but I'm the one who loves your brother. The same person who had a silent crush on him for four years through high school and who only meant to kiss him goodbye. I never intended for anyone to see it. I'm also the person who left a note of apology to Miles up on the water tower to say how sorry I was if I caused any trouble. The same person who put blue dye in the cheerleaders' shampoo—*after* they wrote 'skank' on my locker, *after* they egged me as I walked home from school, and *after* they spilled fruit punch on my white prom dress simply because Tommy Simpson asked me to dance when one of them had a crush on him."

Morgan paused. She hadn't told anyone, even her mother, about the bullying she received in high school. Morgan had always thought of it as her secret embarrassment. She hadn't wanted anyone to feel sorry for her. "Did you know that my perfect sister was the head cheerleader during some of that time?" Before Pierce could interrupt, she felt the story come tumbling out, "And yes, I was disowned. I was disowned because when I came home from graduation, to a party for my sister and her boyfriend that I wasn't invited to, I made the mistake of sitting alone on my porch. How does that turn me into being disowned?"

"From what I've heard you made out with Pam's boyfriend, just like you did with Miles," Pierce said quietly.

Morgan felt another tear slide down her cheek, "I was sexually assaulted by Pam's boyfriend and no one believed me. In fact, everyone *blamed* me." Morgan closed her eyes and told Pierce the story of that afternoon on the porch. She hated to even think about it.

"Why didn't you tell anyone?" Pierce asked gently.

"If my own family didn't believe me, who would have?" Morgan dried her eyes and gave him a half smile. The pain was still fresh after all these years.

"Well, I do. Now tell me, why you think Miles is in danger?" Morgan didn't hesitate this time as she told Pierce the whole story. Pierce stood quietly and listened.

"I believe you and I understand why you need to see Miles." Morgan let out a sigh of relief. It was such a simple statement, but no one had ever believed her before. "Except, we need to do this carefully. I don't want anything to ruin tonight."

"Of course. Believe it or not, I've always liked your family. What do you want me to do?"

Chapter Seventeen

Miles waved his empty glass toward the bartender and waited for him to refill it with red wine. The wedding had been spectacular. He'd never seen his brother so happy. The Wyatts had turned their historic estate into a beautiful wonderland. Tiny white lights shone brightly over the dance floor they had built in the backyard under the magnificent white tent. Beautiful red lanterns hung from the limbs of the massive trees outside and lined the inside of the tent. White lights covered the bushes and smaller trees, while red roses sat on every table.

Unfortunately, all he could think about was seeing Morgan. He wondered what she'd look like in a wedding dress. He took another sip of wine and berated himself for such fanciful thoughts. First he needed to get to the bottom of this and then he'd think about Morgan. He'd been thinking about her so much he actually thought he saw her.

When his mother gasped Miles realized he wasn't hallucinating. "What is she doing here? She's going to ruin everything!"

"Ma, she's not going to ruin anything. I can't believe you'd say something like that." His mother had the good manners to look chagrined.

"Miles!" Pierce waved his hand at his brother when they got closer. The crowd had parted to let them through. "I'm sorry I detained your date. I was just having such a wonderful talk with her that I'm afraid I made her late."

Miles kept his eyes on Morgan as she walked nervously toward him. He felt the rumble in his chest at the sight of her delicate hand on Pierce's arm. All he wanted to do was pull her to him and claim her as his.

"Your *date*?" His mother hissed under her breath. Miles ignored her and rolled his eyes when he saw Paige out of the corner of his eye coming to stand next to his mother as the united female front. Morgan was in for a hard time.

"Hello, sweetheart." Miles reached out and took Morgan's hand away from Pierce and placed it securely in the crook of his arm. "I'm so glad you could make it." He leaned over and kissed her gently and reassuringly on the lips. "Do you know my mother, Marcy? And of course you know my sister." Miles leveled the women in his life with a hard stare as Morgan turned to say hello.

His mother and sister attempted a smile and he watched as Morgan nervously complimented them on their dresses and tried to engage them in conversation. He felt the light poke in his ribs and turned to find Pierce standing grimly behind him.

"We need to talk," Pierce whispered.

Miles nodded and then ordered a glass of white wine for Morgan. As he handed it to her he let his fingers linger on hers and gave her a reassuring smile. "I'll be back in just a minute. I'm trusting you all to take good care of my date." While he said it with a smile he knew his mother and sister heard the command within it.

"Aren't we always nice to all your women?" Paige said too sweetly. Miles narrowed his eyes and his sister just rolled hers. He must've really lost his touch with the intimidating glare he had perfected during his service. He shrugged his shoulders in confusion as he followed Pierce farther into the yard.

Morgan kept a shaky smile on her face as she turned back toward Marcy and Paige. She was totally lost. Miles had played the perfect date but the last time she saw him he'd been irate. Who knew with men?

"Morgan! Don't you look beautiful! I'm so glad you came," Annie smiled warmly as she came to stand next to her. Morgan smiled a real smile and felt such gratitude she was sure Annie could read it in her eyes.

"It's a beautiful wedding. I'm so glad Miles invited me. I'm just sorry I'm late."

"Too busy painting the water tower?" Paige mumbled.

Morgan felt Annie tense up and knew the woman would jump in and defend her if Morgan wanted. She didn't have a chance though. Kenna and Dani came to stand with them and everyone turned to coo over Kenna's sweet little daughter.

"Morgan," Miss Lily said softly from beside her. Morgan jumped a little. She hadn't heard Miss Lily and her Easy Spirits coming. "I wanted to ask you something."

Suddenly her peppy little group went quiet. Even little Sienna, Kenna's daughter, stopped laughing and twirling around nearby on the dance floor. "Yes?" Morgan turned to Miss Lily and hoped to keep the conversation private. She was sure she was going to be reminded of trampling Miss Lily's roses and subsequently getting thwacked with her broom.

"I was wondering, that night I caught you in my roses," Morgan suppressed the desire to clench her teeth together. "What were you doing in my yard?"

Morgan thought about it for a minute and then decided she had nothing to lose. She'd just tell the truth. "My father kicked me out of the house for something I didn't do and I had no place to put my things I stole out of my house before I could hitchhike to Lexington later that night."

"After you committed vandalism and blamed it on my brother," Paige mumbled again.

Morgan drew herself up and looked Paige right in the eye, "Yes, that's right. I did. I couldn't stand to let a chance to get back at Stacy pass me by. It was lame, childish, and wrong. However, I was eighteen, and I'm not eighteen anymore."

Before Paige could respond, Miss Lily put her wrinkled hand on her arm and drew her attention. "I believe I—we—may have been too hard on you. You know, there's nothing wrong with being a rebel. Lord knows I gave my parents a shock once or twice. There was the time I was caught skinny dipping with the hunk next door that turned their hair gray."

Morgan felt her jaw drop and then laughed as she noticed that everyone was staring at Miss Lily slack-jawed. She was still giggling when John Wolfe, the town's most notorious gossip approached them.

"You ladies all look lovely tonight. Miss Lily, will you do me the honor of a dance?" John asked, somewhat embarrassed.

"I'd love to." Miss Lily started to walk away when she turned over her shoulder and gave the group a wink.

Miles followed Pierce into the darkness of the far side of the yard. He had never seen his brother so serious. Miles got a sense that times were changing. Pierce was no longer the gangly band geek from high school. He was a full-grown man now, equal to his older brothers. It was going to be a big adjustment, but Miles realized he needed to start treating Pierce as such.

"What's going on Pierce? Why did you say Morgan was my date?"

"Did you know she had a crush on you in high school?" That wasn't the question he expected.

"I knew. Why?"

"Why didn't you date her?"

"I'm wasn't into girls with multiple arrests. I was more into good wholesome girls then."

"What if I told you Morgan was a good wholesome girl?" Miles just raised one eyebrow. "Okay, not all the way, but underneath the harsh exterior. What if I told you she was nice, good, and loves you?"

"I'd tell you to start talking." Miles crossed his arms over his chest and listened to Pierce tell him about the conversation he had with Morgan.

Miles felt his blood boil as he clenched his fists. Morgan had been bullied her whole life and set up as the troublemaker. She had the guts to stand up to her bullies who then in turn would just get her in more trouble. No wonder she fled Keeneston as soon as she could.

He thought back to his time with Stacy. She had joked about and teased Morgan constantly. He didn't think much of it at the time, but then he'd heard of the pranks they had pulled on her and when he told Stacy how horrible they were for doing so, she had just stopped telling him. He was just as much at fault for what happened as Stacy was. Miles knew about the bullying and he could've done more to stop it.

His pride for her swelled as he thought how she handled this all on her own, all the while keeping her grades high enough to get a full scholarship to college and now she was risking everything to try to protect *him*. She was the strongest, most courageous person he knew.

He looked for her and found her on the dance floor. Then his anger tripled. She was laughing and being twirled around the floor by Henry Rooney. He stalked forward until he felt his arm being grabbed from behind. Turning around he saw his sister with a frown on her face.

"What do you think you're doing? Don't you remember who she is?"

"I know exactly who she is. I'd appreciate it if you stopped being a brat to her and got to know her. I'm sure you'd find that you love her as much as I do." He shot his sister a big grin and went to claim his woman.

Morgan laughed as Henry listed off the reasons they were destined for each other. Once Miss Lily told John Wolfe that Morgan had changed into a responsible woman, the mood shifted. While they were still hesitant about her actions in connection to the fires and poisoning, nobody was running in fear from her either.

Henry suddenly stopped talking and Morgan looked up into his face. It had gone stark white. She turned her head and found Miles glowering at him. He looked fierce in his tuxedo with his hands hanging loosely at his side but enough tension behind his eyes to send chills down her back.

"May I cut in?" Miles may have asked it, but Morgan knew there was no question about it. Henry quickly stepped away and walked to the bar.

"Phew. I thought I had lost my look," Miles joked as he stepped into her arms and started to waltz her around the dance floor to the soft music.

"What look?"

"My intimidation look. Normally it works, but it hasn't worked on you once," Miles puzzled.

"Sorry, but I have a whole lifetime of refusing to be intimidated. Hence, the rebel exterior. But, Miles, I have to tell you something. I'm afraid I really messed up."

"I know you did," Miles whispered as he nuzzled her neck.

"You know? But how could you know I'm stealing files from Top Producers and that they found out and are probably going to try to kill me? You too, most likely, since you won't sell." Morgan's brow was wrinkled in confusion as she looked up at him.

Miles's step faltered and he tightened his grip around her waist to prevent her from tripping. "What? I thought you were talking about us?"

"Us? No, I don't think we've messed up at all. Except for that whole part of you not believing me about hurting those farmers. Which, by the way, I didn't do. I would *never* do." She narrowed her eyes and Miles smiled. She had her own look that would intimidate most people, but he found it too cute.

"Then what is it? Pierce told me what you two talked about already and that you think you're protecting me."

"I didn't tell Pierce everything. The fact of the matter is your life is in danger because of me." Morgan felt Miles stiffen but she forged ahead, "I found out a year ago that David and Top Producers were involved in corporate espionage and other criminal activities. They forced, threatened, and blackmailed their competition into selling to them in the form of what I thought where legitimate mergers." Miles pulled her a little closer and the warmth of his body pressed against hers gave her strength to continue. "Well, last year the president of a company I was closing a deal with said something about hoping David burned in hell for what he did to his secretary. It got me wondering what he was talking about. Late at night after everyone left, I snuck into David's office and read the report he had on the president.

"See, David does two investigations. One through the normal route, and then the second, a more illegal search. He found out the president and secretary were involved in an extramarital affair. They scared the poor woman so much that she ended up committing suicide. The next day the president agreed to the merger." Morgan felt the tears well up even thinking about her part in it. She hadn't known it was going on, but that didn't change anything. She still felt responsible for it.

"That's horrible. What did you do?"

"I told the office I had a doctor's appointment and walked into the lobby of the FBI building. I was assigned an agent who took my report and then said he'd get back to me. I told them I wanted to tell all. I wanted to make sure David paid for his crimes, but the agent said I was a whistleblower and without any direct evidence it was all hearsay. I could get fired and sued for defamation or worse."

"What do you mean, worse?" Miles asked, having a bad feeling where this was headed.

"He said the FBI was now investigating Top Producers and if I didn't get evidence of David's crimes that I would be rounded up in the arrests and charged with the murder of that young woman as a co-conspirator."

"Oh Morgan. Tell me you haven't been gathering evidence all this time. Do you know how dangerous that is?"

"Of course I do. I got the evidence and gave it to the agent the other day at Wal-Mart. But he told me if I didn't get more that I was just as guilty as David and he would leave me to hang with the rest of Top Producers. So, I went back to DC early this morning. I got the evidence. It's now in a safe place, but David caught me in his office. I said I was gathering evidence to hurt you, but I know he knows. I'm just worried he'll take you down with me and I don't know what to do next. I do know I can't trust the FBI."

"Well, I do know someone you can trust." Miles would see Cole first thing in the morning. Tonight was a celebration and he wasn't going to get everyone worried in the middle of a wedding. "We'll talk about it tomorrow. Tonight I want to dance with you and right now I want to kiss you." He loved the way a slight blush highlighted her cheeks.

"Miles, we're in the middle of the dance floor with the whole town around us…"

"Good. Then everyone will know you're mine," he growled as he shot Henry a dirty look. The music slowed to an end and Miles twirled her and then bent her back into a dip. He leaned forward and claimed her lips with his. He momentarily forgot where he was as he stroked his tongue into her mouth, tasting her.

Miles pulled away when he heard the sound of someone clearing his throat. He looked up and saw Marshall smiling down at him with Katelyn standing next to him.

"Oh, um. Congratulations on your wedding," Morgan mumbled in embarrassment.

"Thank you. Although, I don't remember us sending you an invit…"

"Katelyn. I haven't told you the news," Marshall interrupted as Morgan felt her face turn bright red in embarrassment. "Morgan is Miles's plus one. She couldn't make it to the wedding, but said she was honored to be invited to the reception."

Morgan was mortified. Here stood a beautiful woman with her blonde hair pinned up and a long veil hanging over her bare shoulders, wearing a gorgeous dress complete with a sweetheart neckline flowing down into a tight fit before exploding into a cloud of ruffles at her knees. She was breathtaking and here was Morgan, uninvited, wearing a dirty martini.

"That's nice. Are you two dating then?" Katelyn asked clearly confused.

"No. Yes," they said at the same time. Miles gave her a look and then turned to his brother and new sister-in-law and smiled. "Yes, we are. This is our what, third date, love?"

With her eyes wide, Morgan looked back and forth between the family members, "Yes it is. We were just keeping it quiet, that's all."

"I don't think you are anymore," Katelyn laughed.

Maybe she didn't hate her? Morgan couldn't tell and she really wished she could. There was nothing she wanted more than to not embarrass Miles, starting with his family liking her. "I guess not. Um, Katelyn?" Morgan paused not really knowing what to say. "Thank you. You two make a wonderful couple and I wish you much happiness."

Katelyn looked Morgan over, trying to decide what to believe. Finally she smiled and nodded, "Thank you Morgan. Well, we're off to make the rounds. You two have fun."

"I plan on having a lot of fun tonight," Miles whispered into her ear causing her to blush for a whole other reason.

Chapter Eighteen

Miles stood next to Morgan as they waved goodbye to Marshall and Katelyn. His brother and his new wife ran down the stone path toward their limousine. Miles could feel Morgan's shoulder rubbing against his body as she smiled at the happy couple. He had to touch more of her. He slid his hand over hers and pulled it in close to his lips. Miles looked down at her and smiled before placing a soft kiss on her hand.

"Let's go," Miles whispered in her ear while the crowd around them cheered and waved.

Morgan could only nod as she allowed Miles to pull her along through the people to his car. She suddenly felt self-conscious as she sat waiting for Miles to jog around the car. She just had a hard time believing all this was happening. It was hard to not get lost in her feelings for Miles, but could she afford to?

When his hand squeezed her knee and started to massage its way up her leg she decided she could definitely afford it. In fact she'd felt as if she'd been saving for it her whole life. She looked over at Miles and found him looking at her with such heat in his eyes she felt as if she'd melt into the seat.

"Miles, don't you think we should talk about David?" she asked, nearly breathless.

"No. Not tonight." She felt his hand bunch up her long dress and pull it up over her knees. Her breath caught when his fingers danced along her thigh and headed for her…

"Oh. My. God." Morgan panted as his fingers traced along her panty line. She closed her eyes and leaned her head back and burned with every touch of his fingers.

"We're here," she heard his husky voice say through her haze of passion.

"Not yet. Keep going!" Morgan's eyes shot open when she heard Miles's low laughter.

"No, I mean we're at my house," he chuckled as he turned off his car.

Morgan took a couple deep breaths as Miles made his way to her door while she tried to calm herself down. She was afraid she might not make it to the bedroom if she didn't. His hands—his fingers!

Miles opened the door. When she looked up at his outstretched hand, then up the muscled arm to his chiseled face, she lost what little control she had. Morgan placed her hand in his and stood up. She took a step forward and stumbled on the brick walkway. His arms wrapped around her to steady her and she looked up into his hazel eyes now darkened with pleasure.

Oh screw calming down! Morgan wrapped her hands around his neck and brought his lips to hers. She gently rubbed her lips against his and then softly sucked on his lower lip. Miles pulled her possessively against him and stroked his tongue against hers slowly. She let out a groan in frustration—she wanted more. She had to have more!

Morgan deepened the kiss and ran her hands down his back. She ground against him until she felt his manhood grow hard in response. Before Morgan knew it, her dress was unzipped and sliding to the ground. Morgan felt the cool night air dance along her heated skin as she tossed her head back and looked at the stars.

"Much better," Miles mumbled into her neck as he started to trail kisses down her throat. His hands teased her nipples into pleasured peaks.

Morgan wasted no time herself. He wasn't going to have all the fun. As they stumbled up the path toward the house she stripped him of this tuxedo jacket and clumsily managed to unbutton his shirt. Her feet hit the bottom stair of the porch and Miles guided her down to the steps.

He knelt before her and looked up sensually at her, "I want you, here, now," he practically growled as he placed a kiss on that sensitive spot behind her knee.

She was about to respond when he moved up her leg with his lips and then suddenly the stairs seemed like the perfect place to… "OhMyGod!" she screamed into the night air.

Morgan snuggled closer to Miles as they lay curled up in bed. They had finally made it inside and then up to the bedroom after a quick layover on the hall rug. Miles was stroking her hair as she absently ran her fingers over his chest. She couldn't be any happier. They fit together perfectly—in more ways than one.

"Miles, I was thinking about something." She moved her head back on his arm so she could look up at him. "What do you think about…" She was cut off by Bill whose head lifted from his big dog bed on the floor. Gone was the sweet old dog with big round eyes. Bill's hair rose and he was baring his teeth as he growled at her. "Miles, why is he growling at me?"

"It's not you. I hear the geese too," Miles said tightly as he pulled his arm out from under her to go look out the window.

"So?"

"It means we're not alone." Miles pulled back the curtain just enough to be able to see out. "Crap! They're coming. Put this on." Miles tossed her his tuxedo shirt as he grabbed his pants off the floor.

"Who is?" Morgan asked in confusion. She pulled the large shirt over her head, buttoning the top couple of buttons. The shirt was long enough to come slightly above her knees.

"David's friends. Hurry!"

Miles yanked her from the bed as he pulled a handgun from one of the dresser drawers. "Here. Do you know how to use this?" Morgan shook her head. Her parents had never allowed guns in the house. "I turned the safety off, so don't aim it at anything unless you intend to pull the trigger."

Miles shoved the gun in her hand. She was surprised how heavy it felt. Bill trotted along her side as Miles pulled her down the stairs as fast as he could. "Where are we going?"

"We aren't going anywhere. You are. I'm going to get their attention. I want you to run as fast as you can out the back door and into the woods. Follow the moon and it'll take you to my parents' house."

"I can't leave you here!" Morgan worried. She wanted to stay with Miles to keep him safe; she couldn't imagine leaving him behind.

"You can and you will. Please, Morgan. I'll be able to do my job a lot better without worrying about you." Miles opened the gun safe hidden in a large cabinet and pulled out an M-16 and another handgun, which he shoved into his waistband at the small of his back. He turned back to her and Morgan felt the tears start to fall.

"Please," she begged.

"Morgan, you need to do this for me, okay?" Morgan nodded slowly then. If it was better for him, then she'd do it. "I'm going to go upstairs. As soon as you hear the first shot, run with all you have." Morgan looked down on her bare feet and grimaced. She only had four-inch heels—not too good for running.

"I love you. I always have." Morgan ran her hand over the stubble on his cheek.

"I know. Get ready." Miles bent down and gave her a searing kiss that lasted only a second. All too soon he was bounding up the stairs.

She looked down at Bill who gave her a little whine and walked to the back door with her.

"I guess it's just you and me." Bill thumped his tail and Morgan unlocked the door and waited.

Morgan tried to stay calm in order to hear Miles's cue over her beating heart. She wondered if she'd know it when she heard it. She looked down at Bill who sat calmly by her feet. This was all her fault. All of it. It seemed like a good idea until she placed Miles square in the middle of danger.

A shot rang out and Morgan said a quick prayer for his safety as she ripped open the door and took off at a dead run. She kept her eyes on the tree line as her feet padded over the well-manicured lawn. Bill stuck to her side as she blindly sprinted forward. She plowed into the hidden depths of the trees and bushes and felt the pain first on her feet as the soft grass turned to dead leaves and sticks. Then she was faced with the problem of constantly being hit on the face, arms, and body as she pushed through shrubs and darted around large evergreens.

Bill growled but she didn't have time to think what it meant as a body hit her. She gasped for breath as she was being flung into a leafless bush. Her hands landed first as she tried to block her fall, but with the man on top of her it made the impact worse. The gun she'd been carrying went flying out of her hand. When she hit the ground she felt the last of her air being stolen from her lungs as the man's full weight came down on her.

Bill barked madly as a hand came up to tangle itself in her hair. She tried to scream when the man pulled hard yanking her head up from the ground. "You're dead, bitch," the man snarled before pushing her face back into the cold ground.

Morgan fought for breath until she felt the weight removed from her back. She breathed deeply, coughing and sputtering out the dirt in her mouth. She thought Miles had come until she felt her head being yanked back. She staggered to a standing position to lessen the pain as she looked around wildly.

Bill was dancing madly around them as the man held her against his body. Miles was nowhere to be found. He wasn't going to save her. The sad realization hit her as she felt the man's hands wrap around her throat. That left only one option—she was just going to have to save herself.

Morgan struggled to fill her lungs with air and garnering all the strength she had, she flung her elbow backward toward the man's gut. She heard him grunt and loosen his hands around her throat enough for her to break his hold. Not waiting to see what he'd do next, Morgan tried to run but the man had managed to snag her shirt.

"Going somewhere, pet?" His menacing voice turned her blood to ice. She dug her heels into the ground and used all her weight to try to force him to lose his grip on her shirt. Instead the man let go and she stumbled forward, landing on her knee. A branch from a tree hit her in the face as she reached out to try to save herself from falling completely to the ground.

"Feisty, aren't we?" he laughed. Morgan took a breath and hung her head in defeat. She waited until the man stood in front of her and then launched herself at him. Fists flew and she connected but couldn't tell where. Pain shot up her arm as she continued the assault.

The man wrenched her hand that was clawing at his face. Before she could protect herself, she felt the back of his hand hit her. Pain blossomed and spread across her face. Tears sprang involuntarily from her eyes and she felt blood drip from her nose and down her split lip. She suddenly understood the meaning of "having your bell rung."

"You think that's going to break me you dumb son of a bitch?" Morgan wiped the blood from her face and smiled. She widened her grin when she saw his confidence falter momentarily.

Out of the corner of her eye she saw the gun Miles had given her lying on the ground. Taking advantage of his brief hesitation Morgan lunged for the gun. She felt him reach out to grab her. The side of the shirt ripped under his grasp causing her to fall short of the gun. It was just a foot away, but the man in black was standing over her now. She had blown her one chance.

"It's almost a shame I have to kill you," he seethed.

Morgan rolled over and looked up at the man.

"Too bad almost doesn't count in life or death." He pulled out a gun and aimed it at her as he stood over her, clearly enjoying her fear.

Bill bayed as he nipped at the man's ankles. The man just kicked him away. Bill cried out in pain as the man's kick connected and sent him through the air.

Rage overtook Morgan. The man was still laughing at the dog's injury when Morgan used every ounce of her strength to kick her leg up and bust his balls.

"Son of a bitch!" the man gasped, as he grabbed his injured boys and bent over taking deep breaths.

Morgan pushed herself forward and grabbed the gun. She fumbled with it as she turned and aimed up toward the man. He looked up and in shock, aimed his gun at her, and went to fire, but not before Morgan pulled the trigger twice. The man fell to his knees. Eyes full of anger and shock locked with hers before he fell face-first into the ground at her feet.

Morgan scrambled to her feet and rushed over to Bill. "You're such a good boy. Let's get out of here." Fearing to release the dog that saved her life, Morgan scooped Bill up and stumbled forward with him in her arms. She picked up her pace and jogged through the trees. Sticks and branches were hitting her as she ran past them, no longer recognizing the slicing pain.

Morgan pushed through a row of boxwood bushes and stumbled onto a dirt road. She heard tires slide on dirt as brakes were slammed. Bright lights suddenly blinded her as she struggled to hold Bill.

"Jesus H. Christ," she heard a man say.

Morgan held the dog close and aimed the gun. She could see a man approaching her. "Stop or I'll shoot you."

"Morgan? It's Pierce. Put that down!"

"Pierce?" Morgan gasped.

"What happened to you?" Morgan dropped to her knees, the exhaustion overtaking her. Bill whimpered and kissed her face. "Come on, let's get you to my mom's house," he said gently.

Morgan felt him try to lift the dog out of her arms, but when she refused to let go he lifted them together, carrying them to his truck. "No! You have to help Miles! Just leave me here!" He tucked her safely into his truck and quickly turned it around and headed up the dirt road.

"What's going on Morgan?"

She was starting to get irritated with his calm voice. "The men I told you about, they came! Miles tried to hold them off so I could escape, but one of the men found me in the woods." Pierce didn't ask what happened and Morgan was grateful for that. She felt as if she was living this experience outside of her own body. "Please, help Miles!" Morgan felt the tears start to trickle down her cheeks.

"I will. I don't have anything to help him with in the truck. I'm going to do what my brother would want me to do—get you someplace safe first." Morgan choked back tears as images of life without Miles filled her mind. She barely heard Pierce on the phone with Cade and some guy named Ahmed. Somewhere in the back of her mind she remembered that name associated with security. She doubted some security guard would be much help and the tears started anew.

By the time the large farmhouse came into view Marcy was standing in the driveway alongside her husband. Rifles leaned against the stairs, causing a coldness crept into her again. Shivers wracked her body. Pierce slid the truck to a stop and Jake was at her door instantly.

"I'm so sorry. It's all my fault," she whimpered as he helped her out. Marcy wrapped her in a blanket and it was only then that she looked down and saw only two buttons remained on the shirt that was covered in blood and dirt. A sleeve was ripped and by the draft she was feeling, the tail of the shirt was also ripped off.

"It's okay, dear. Jake and Pierce will take care of it." Morgan heard the desperation in her voice. Pierce and Jake tore out of the driveway before she even had the chance to reach the first step.

"I'm so sorry Mrs. Davies. I'm the reason your son is in danger and if anything happens to him it's all my fault," Morgan cried. Sobs wracked her body as she felt Marcy guide her up the stairs. She glanced at the strong woman next to her and when Morgan saw tears silently falling from Marcy's eyes she tried to control her own tears. Marcy was taking care of her while worried for her family's safety.

"Here," Marcy guided her to the couch in the living room, "let me take Bill."

"No!" Morgan gripped the sturdy little dog in her arms. She couldn't explain it, but she felt that Bill was her link to Miles and she was never going to let go.

"Okay. I'll go get you some ice for your face." Morgan stared after her and curled up into a little ball.

"Miles, please come back to me," she whispered into Bill's coat as she held him tight against her chest.

Miles closed and locked the door to his bedroom. He carried the guns to the window, propped them against the wall, and laid out the ammunition in a neat row. He pressed the panic button on his alarm on the way to his closet. He pulled and pushed some boxes out of the way and reached up for the large duffle bag, which he placed next to the window. He pulled out his Delta Force knife and strapped it to the side of his pants.

"There you are," Miles pulled out a night scope and attached it to the rifle. Before he got the chance to open the curtains and evaluate the situation further gunfire erupted.

The glass shattered but Miles sat back and waited. The sound of the bullets ripping apart his house pissed him off. He felt the familiar rage gathering and let it come. His hearing intensified and his vision sharpened as he picked up the rifle. He looked out the window. Calmly he started taking out the men in black that were surrounding the house.

One made a dash for the front door and Miles pulled the trigger. He scanned the tree line counting the men. He quickly moved to the back and counted more men coming out of the woods.

He took two quick shots and rushed down the stairs. He had to go after Morgan and protect her if it wasn't too late already. He rushed to the bedroom door when he heard an explosion below. Miles slowly crept down the hall with his M-16 snug against his shoulder. The front door was gone and through the smoke of the small charge he saw a figure slowly making his way inside.

Miles took a steadying breath and waited patiently for the man to come into full view before pulling the trigger. "I really liked my door, asshole," Miles mumbled as he hurried down the stairs.

He pushed his large credenza from the dining room to block the door before racing back upstairs. He did a quick grid scan of the backyard and saw a total of three men converging. He picked off two, but one managed to seek protection behind his stone fire pit.

Miles rushed across the large room to the front window. They just kept coming! Before he could get a shot off, he heard a crash as the large window was shattered by a spray of bullets. He looked for the culprit and finally found him sitting in the maple tree out front.

Miles didn't know how much longer he would be able to hold them off. He just hoped the silent alarm would send help soon. He pushed aside the curtain no longer trying to hide his actions and laid ground cover to prevent the men in front from advancing. Miles checked the back yard and found it empty. The man had made it into the house.

Miles crept slowly to the door and cracked it open. The door was kicked open and smashed against his face, knocking him backwards. Miles didn't wait to see who came through before he roared and charged the figured lurking behind the door. Their bodies connected and went tumbling backward down the hallway.

He felt the man land next to him as Miles scrambled to his feet. He kicked the man's gun down the hall before placing a well-aimed kick to the man's gut. Miles reached down, grabbed the man by his Kevlar vest and hauled him to his feet.

"Tell David to send more men next time," Miles growled as he shook the man.

"You're never going to make it out alive," the man sneered from under his black ski mask. In one quick motion he reached for his waist and produced a sharp blade.

Miles heard the sound of the knife being drawn and didn't wait. He pulled the man close to him and with all his strength sent the man in black sailing over the banister and crashing to the floor below. Unfortunately he lost his human shield and the sniper fire started again. Miles was forced to dive to the ground as bullets riddled the wall where his head had been just seconds ago.

Miles crawled on his stomach to his bedroom. He hurried when he heard the additional gunfire added into the mix. The mercenaries must have called for reinforcements.

"Drop your weapons and come out with your hands up!" Miles stopped in his tracks. What the hell? He looked around and noticed the gunfire had stopped. He hurried to the window and looked outside. "That means you too, you sorry piece of..."

"Annie?" Miles yelled out the window as he stared at his sister-in-law standing next to the Keeneston sheriff department's SUV with her gun in one hand, holding a bullhorn in the other.

"Oh, hey. Glad to see you're still alive." Annie quickly raised her handgun and shot off into the dark. Miles heard a yelp and knew she had just hit one of the attackers. "Do you know how hard it is to get a baby to sleep? I finally got her down and you bastards woke me up! Is everyone good now?" She shouted into the bullhorn.

Miles watched as he saw Ahmed and some men he recognized as Ahmed's security team, Noodle, Dinky, Cade, Pierce, Cole and his father coming from all directions leading men in black with their hands up. He had only seen ten or so but there were at least twice as many now. He'd never have been able to hold them all off. Thank God his crew had arrived when they did.

"Morgan?" Miles shouted out the window as he scrambled to his feet.

"She's okay. I picked her up and left her in Ma's care," Pierce called back as he strode forward with the barrel of his gun trained on the man walking in front of him.

Miles released the breath he was holding. He grabbed a shirt from the closet and stuffed his feet into some shoes before running down the stairs and heading out onto the front yard.

"I've called in my team and they'll be here soon to collect these men," Cole told Miles when he met them outside. "But Miles, they're telling me it was a woman named Morgan who hired them."

"I don't believe it. I need to see her." Miles was anxiously eyeing his car sitting near the barn. He could barely make himself stand still. He needed to make sure she was safe in his arms.

"I think we all need to talk to Morgan," Cole told the group.

Chapter Nineteen

Morgan clutched Bill to her chest as Marcy wrapped another blanket around her. Paige sat quietly across the room from her, but Morgan barely noticed. She couldn't stop shaking. All she could think about was Miles. He couldn't be dead, he just couldn't be.

"It's okay sweetie. We'll hear something soon," Marcy cooed trying to calm herself just as much as Morgan. "What happened, Morgan?"

"It's all my fault. Everything is my fault," Morgan cried as she buried her head into Bill's soft fur again.

"Morgan!"

Morgan raised her head and saw Miles rushing through the door. He was a mess, but he was alive! Bruises were starting to blossom on his face as he hurried to her side.

"Miles! You're alive!"

"Is that good or bad?" Cole asked.

Morgan only tossed him a confused glance as she put a squirming Bill on the floor and opened her arms to him. Miles pulled her into his arms and crushed her against his chest. She grimaced at the pain but didn't dare say anything. He was alive and that was all that mattered.

"I'm so sorry Miles, it's all my fault. If it wasn't for me this wouldn't have happened. I didn't think David would move this fast," she cried into his chest as she squeezed him reassuring herself that he was really there.

"See, she admits it. I told you she was nothing but trouble!"

"Paige..." Miles warned his sister.

"Morgan," Cole interrupted. "We haven't officially met, but I'm Special Agent Cole Parker of the FBI. I think it's time we talked."

Morgan stiffened and her head nearly hit Miles in the jaw as she stood to face Cole. "I don't think so. I won't talk to the FBI without an attorney present." Morgan thought of her dealings with Agent Breton and anger replaced her fear.

"Most of the time that's what guilty people say," Cole casually commented.

"Or people who are sick of dealing with lying FBI scumbags," Morgan shot back, moving her hands to her hips as Miles pulled the blanket tight to cover her.

Cole narrowed his eyes at her, "You've been dealing with the FBI?" he asked.

"I'm not saying another word until I get a lawyer. Isn't Henry from high school a lawyer?" she asked Miles.

"Yes. Come into the kitchen and you can give him a call."

Morgan paced around the kitchen and waited for her attorney to arrive. She could only hope Henry was as smart as he was in high school and that he had lost the swagger that didn't quite fit with his personality.

The door to the kitchen opened and a rather disheveled Henry strode in with a briefcase in hand. "Miles, can someone get my client something to wear?"

Miles looked at her for permission to leave and she gave a slight nod of her head.

"Now that we're alone..."

"Oh God Henry, not a pick up line," she mumbled as she pulled the blanket tighter around her.

"Sorry, but I reserve those lines for special women who aren't my clients—even if you beg." Henry smiled and she felt herself relax. The door opened and Miles came in with jeans and a blue University of Kentucky sweatshirt. "Thanks Miles. Now if you'll excuse us I need to speak privately with my client."

Once again Morgan nodded her approval and waited for Miles to leave. Henry came over to her and stopped in front of her, "You'll feel better once you change. I'll go talk to Cole and be back in just a minute. Is there anything else you need?"

"No. And Henry, thank you so much." Henry smiled and headed out the door. She ripped off the torn dress shirt and pulled on the warm sweatshirt. She tugged on the jeans and had to leave the top button undone, but at least the sweatshirt hid the fact that she couldn't fit into the jeans.

Henry knocked on the door and entered when she told him it was okay. He took out a notepad and a computer and sat down at the kitchen table with her. "Okay. Start at the beginning and don't leave anything out."

Morgan took a deep breath and started with getting her job at Top Producers. Henry took notes and asked follow-up questions as she told her story. Before she knew it she was lost in the nightmare of her race to get back and warn Miles.

Miles paced the living room floor as his mother sat next to his father nervously wringing her hands together. Annie had left to relieve Tammy of babysitting duty. Cade and Pierce were sitting in the corner with their legs stretched out in front of them looking as if they didn't have a care in the world. Miles narrowed his eyes at them but was distracted when Cole got up to answer a phone call. He moved out onto the porch and Miles instantly became suspicious.

"I don't understand this, Miles. You're usually such a good judge of character," Paige pushed at him again. She was his little sister and he loved her, but God help him, she had a bug up her craw about Morgan and he was tired of it.

"Paige, I thought we had this discussion. Why don't you like her?" Miles asked through a clenched jaw.

"She hurt you and you were never the same after that."

"That's right, me—not you! I've moved on, why can't you? And I still have good judgment. It's the only reason I let your husband near her. Because I trust him, like you should trust me. When you learn what's going on, you're going to be redder than a pickled beet and I expect an apology from you." Miles dropped his hands from his hips and strode back across the room. He could feel her eyes roll, but then the front door opened and Cole came in with his cop face on. Miles knew there was going to be trouble.

"Miles, a word please?" Cole opened the front door and Miles dutifully walked out on to the porch.

"What is it?"

"Did you know Morgan was being investigated by the FBI for fraud, embezzlement, illegal lobbying, intimidation, and murder?" Cole's expression didn't change.

"That asshole! David Washington is behind this." Miles's fingers clinched into a fist. He was going to kill that SOB.

"I'm going to have to bring her in for questioning and will most likely have to arrest her tonight. The evidence is there, but for some reason the agent in charge hasn't pushed for a warrant yet." Cole opened the door and went inside leaving Miles staring out into the early morning light.

Morgan took another sip of water as she waited. Henry was bent over his computer typing away at the document that would determine the rest of her life. He had been a good listener and grasped the situation quicker than she thought possible. If the Keeneston Belles could see him like this—serious, scholarly lawyer—he would be at the top of the most eligible list faster than John Wolfe could spread gossip.

"I think I have it. Read this over and let me know what you think." Henry turned the computer over to her as she read through her lifeline.

"Good. Thanks again Henry. Do you think you can prevent me from going to jail?" Morgan asked nervously.

"Let's find out. Are you ready?" Henry printed off the report on Marcy and Jake's printer and put his arm around her shoulder to lead the way into the living room.

All conversation stopped as she walked through the door. The mixture of reactions would've been humorous if not for the situation. Miles hurried through the door and took his place by her side in a show of support. Morgan's heart clenched, thinking she might not see the man she loved again. Her life was in the hands of Henry.

"Henry, I'm sorry, but I got word on your client. I need to take her to the FBI office and have a talk with her. If she refuses I'm going to have to arrest her." Cole told him as he pulled out a pair of cuffs. Morgan gasped, but then she felt both Miles and Henry's reassuring touch.

"I think you're going to want to hear what she says first." Henry stopped Cole's movement toward her by handing out the pages he'd just printed off.

"What's this?" Cole looked over the document. His eyes widened and he looked straight at Morgan, "A Witness Cooperation Agreement? You'll testify against David Washington and other unnamed people in exchange for no charges being brought against you for any acts you've preformed while an employee at Top Producers? What the hell is this about? Do you really think I'll sign this not knowing the details and not seeing any proof of their so-called criminal activities while the evidence I've seen all points to you?"

"I thought you would say that." Henry pulled out another piece of paper and handed it to Cole. "Here's a list of crimes she has witnessed and has evidence for."

Cole let out a breath and ran his hand over his hair. Morgan tightened her grip on Miles's hand and said a quick prayer. "Okay. If your client answers all my questions to my satisfaction and provides evidence for such, then we'll see about signing that agreement."

"Only if it's off the record." Henry took the paper back and stared down Cole.

"Fine." Cole looked to Miles, "This is only because of you and you will so owe me. Start talking Morgan."

Morgan felt her hands trembling as she let go of his hand and took a breath. Miles and Henry had assured her that Cole was a good man and agent, but it was hard to believe after what she'd just seen.

"I'm a whistleblower," she said simply. She heard Marcy gasp and saw Paige's eyes go wide.

"How so?" Cole asked.

"I became aware of illegal activities at Top Producers that resulted in the suicide of a woman."

"Knowing that and failing to do anything about it doesn't make you a whistleblower. In fact it makes you an accessory after the fact." Cole's eyes narrowed and Morgan knew he thought her guilty.

"I did do something. I went to the FBI and reported it."

"Don't lie to me! I have your file right here and you're the prime suspect!" Cole tossed the file onto the table and watched her.

"I talked for hours with Agent Brenton of the DC office. He told me it wasn't enough. He told me I had to provide evidence before I was able to receive immunity under the Whistleblower Act. So I got it. I've already given it to Agent Brenton. But he told me it wasn't enough. It was never enough. I've been providing evidence to the FBI for over a year. Now my life is in danger and the FBI wants to hang me out to dry instead of helping me!" Morgan screamed. She had done everything and they still wanted more.

"What did you supposedly provide Agent Brenton?" Cole asked quietly.

Morgan took several deep breaths to keep the tears from breaking free before she answered, "I have emails between David

Washington and his head of security, William Brady, ordering the blackmail that led to the death of the woman. I have reports and notes by Washington and his security team detailing specifically what pieces of information they dug up on shareholders to use as blackmail. Locations where family members of shareholders lived with names circled of who was to be threatened—in one case the address was a school where the president's seven-year-old daughter attended. I copied them onto a flash drive and handed it to Brenton. He told me it wasn't enough, that I was going to jail for all of this if I didn't get more information even though I had fulfilled all the obligations to become a protected whistleblower."

"What did you do?" Cole started to rub the scruff on his chin and Morgan was worried that he didn't believe her.

"I got more evidence."

"More?"

"Yes. I got bank statements showing a payout of $100,000 to a group that was previously mentioned in the emails. I also found voice recordings. David was paranoid and taped some of his conversations with some powerful people—I'm sure to use as blackmail at some point in the future."

"Brenton was the agent on the file. Why should I believe you?" Cole narrowed his eyes and she felt him searching her face for signs of her character.

"Because I still have a copy of all the evidence Brenton requested along with my own voice recordings of my meetings with Brenton."

"Let me see the evidence," Cole commanded.

"I'm sorry Agent Parker," Henry interrupted. "You'll need to sign this immunity document if you want to see that evidence." Cole cursed and held up a finger to signal for them to wait. He pulled out his cell phone and headed for the porch once again.

Miles pulled her close to him and she didn't even realize how cold she was until she felt his warmth as he held her.

"Shh. It's okay. Cole will get the bottom of this. Even though I want to kill him, I know he's doing his job and he does it well."

The room was quiet and Morgan felt everyone staring at her. Did they believe her? She was about to plead her innocence again when Cole walked back in the door.

"I talked to my superior, Agent Salmonds, and he agreed to me signing the agreement."

"Thank you!" Morgan cried, feeling the tears fall. This nightmare was almost over. At least she wouldn't spend the rest of her life in a jail cell for something she didn't do.

"Don't thank me yet. Let's see this evidence. Where is it?" Cole asked as he handed the signed document back to Henry.

"The safest place I know," Morgan grinned through her tears of relief.

Chapter Twenty

Morgan pointed across the street and Cole just stared. Paige giggled from the back seat and she heard Miles hide a laugh under the pretense of a cough. Cole just kept staring and Marcy smiled from where she sat next to Paige.

"You'll find a silver horse under there in a plastic bag. It's a flash drive with all the evidence on it," Morgan told him. Cole shrugged his shoulders and opened the door to his SUV.

"Be careful!" Marcy called after him. "That really was very clever. Morgan, I'm sorry that we've misjudged you all these years. I hope you give us a chance to get to know you."

"Thank you Mrs. Davies." Morgan watched as Cole jogged across the street and up the walkway of the old white Victorian house. He counted the rose bushes and got down on his hands and knees to crawl under the fifth one.

"Oh no. He's going to be caught!" Paige laughed. While Paige wasn't openly friendly to her, at least she wasn't being mean anymore.

Morgan watched in terror as the front door to the house opened and Miss Lily appeared with her broom. "I told him he should've rung the bell to tell her what he was doing." Morgan shook her head.

Miss Lily crept down the stairs and stopped behind Cole where the only thing sticking out of her prized rose bushes were his legs and perfectly shaped bottom. The perfectly shaped bottom that just got thwacked by a broom!

"Get out of my roses your hoodlum!" Morgan heard Miss Lily yell before bringing the broom down on his bottom again and again.

"Oh God! This is the funniest thing I've ever seen." Paige laughed.

Morgan even managed a smile as Cole came out from under the bushes with his hands up. Miss Lily was berating him up one side and down the other for messing with her bushes. Cole tried to cut in and pointed to the car. Miss Lily peered in and with a nod headed toward them.

"Someone's in trouble," Miles teased. "I think Cole told on you for hiding things in her bushes." Morgan cracked a smile when she saw the small horse dangling from Cole's fingers. It was safe and she was free!

Miss Lily leaned into the car window. "What's going on here?" She thumped her broom against the road like a trident and Morgan tried not to laugh.

"I'm sorry, Miss Lily. I told Cole he should've knocked. He was just retrieving something I hid in your bushes."

Cole pulled out his laptop and inserted the flash drive.

"Why would you do that? When did you do that? I would've seen you if you tried to hide anything."

"I wasn't a delinquent for nothing," Morgan fought back the old animosity.

"Pish posh. I'm starting to believe you were a delinquent as much as I believe Violet never uses precut apples in her pie."

"Holy sh…" Thwack! Miss Lily's broom landed square on Cole's bottom. "Sorry ma'am. Morgan, I owe you an apology too. We might all need to apologize—profusely" Cole looked to Paige before grabbing his cell phone. "I need to call my boss." Cole walked away with the laptop in one hand as he talked into the phone.

"What's going on here? What was the horse doing in my garden and why is Cole calling his boss?" Morgan rolled her eyes. They were cornered and Miss Lily had her broom—she'd beat it out of them if they didn't tell her.

Marcy, bless her heart, filled Miss Lily in on the details. Morgan watched as Miss Lily grunted once, but didn't seem surprised. "I'm glad we talked at the wedding. I heard all about the arrests last night. You two are good together. Now if you'll excuse me, I need to get down to the café."

Morgan watched Miss Lily hurry down the street with her broom. "What's she in such a hurry for?"

"I'm guessing she has a bet to place on a wedding date," Marcy said as she started to rummage around her purse for something.

"But Marshall got married last night. Isn't she a little late?" Morgan asked as Cole started to walk back to the car.

"Not Marshall dear. Oh! Here it is!" Marcy pulled out a twenty and smiled. "Thank goodness they took Mo's private jet out last night or they would've been stuck here with all this mess. Not that you're a mess, dear. In fact, I'm growing rather fond of you. Don't you think long engagements are silly? When you're in love, you're in love. Jake and I waited three weeks to get married, you know?"

"What?" Morgan was totally lost at this point.

"I talked to Salmonds. I told him what I found and he needs to talk to you in person at some point. He also looked over your file and into Agent Brenton. Apparently Brenton is up for a big promotion and was using this case to make his career. Instead it's going to break his career. Salmonds is personally handling his discipline. I looked at it more carefully and now it's clear you were being set up to take the fall. I'm going to bet those emails to the mercenaries were sent from your work computer while you were here with all of us as witnesses. Yet, you went back time after time and with no regard for your safety to get enough evidence to lock David Washington and his goons up for the rest of their lives. When looking at all this, it's clear you never participated in anything illegal, so why did you do it? Why did you get all this evidence and risk your life to expose these people?" Cole looked at her with astonishment and Morgan knew the ordeal was finally over. She didn't have to pretend anymore.

"It was actually quite simple. It was the right thing to do. I never liked causing trouble. I only did it when I was younger to get my father's attention. When I saw what David was doing—the pain he was inflicting on others, I just couldn't stand it. I thought it was my duty to help those people."

"That's very noble of you, Morgan." Marcy patted her on her shoulder and then looked at the large group. "Why don't we all go down to the café and have breakfast together? We can start talking about our future together instead of focusing on the past. Besides, I need to speak with Daisy Mae about something."

Morgan's stomach rumbled in response and Miles lifted an eyebrow at her. "I think that settles that question. Breakfast first then we'll tackle correcting the past misconceptions and moving forward." Morgan's stomach flipped for a whole other reason when Miles squeezed her thigh in support.

Morgan and the group entered the café and found Miss Lily standing in the middle of the room with her broom tilted threateningly at John Wolfe's portly stature. In fact, the patrons were so engrossed in the scene that they didn't even notice that the infamous Morgan Hamilton had entered.

"What's going on?" Morgan whispered to Miles.

"I don't know. But it seems riveting. I can't look away... is she going to hit him or not? Is he going to hit her with his belly and send her flying across the room?"

Morgan agreed. She couldn't stop watching as the broom got closer and closer to John's face.

"I'm telling you I'm the first one who said we needed to admit we made a mistake about Morgan. That she wasn't the same pierced and dyed delinquent that she was in high school. *And,* I'm the one who said maybe she wasn't as bad in high school as we made her out to be." Miss Lily leaned threatening closer to John's red face.

"If you ain't lying you ain't breathin'! I was the first one to tell them that. It was me who got the scoop on you! I knew the second the mercenaries drove into town. How do you think Dinky and Noodle got there so fast? You beat that, woman!" John leaned down and brought his face near Miss Lily's.

"I know she's working with the FBI and has been this whole time in order to right the wrongs of her company. That she's riskin' her life for justice. Now beat that you old billy goat!" Miss Lily smirked as she poked John in the chest. Her perfectly coiffed hair had fallen slightly on her run from her house to the café to spread the gossip she'd had just learned about Morgan.

Morgan couldn't take her eyes away the scene. The broom was so close and John and Miss Lily were toe-to-toe. John leaned forward and placed his lips on Miss Lily's. The patrons gave a collective gasp. Morgan felt her eyes go wide and her chin nearly hit the floor along with everyone else's.

"That'll shut you up," John murmured into the shocked silence.

THWAK! Miss Lily's broom came down hard over John's head. Pieces of straw went flying and there was now a big crack along the broom's handle. Miss Lily spun on one heel, put her nose up in the air, and sauntered out of the café as John smiled after her.

"Well. Morgan, I do believe you're no longer a novelty after that display. So, how about breakfast? I do love the steak and eggs," Marcy said as she took a seat at one of the round tables.

Morgan looked around and almost laughed at what she saw. No one was bothering her. They were all gossiping about John finally making a move on Miss Lily.

"After all, his wife had died almost ten years ago…"

"Miss Lily should finally get over that boy."

"They bonded over gossip."

"Maybe she'll finally learn how he finds things out before anyone else. I still think it's aliens."

It was a wonderful feeling to sit down without the whole restaurant looking at her and knowing that for once the whispers weren't about her.

Miles held out a chair and Morgan sat down. Marcy and Jake sat across from her. Paige and Cole sat between Miles and Jake. The bell rang over the door and Pierce strode in. He looked around and smiled when he saw the group.

"I had to give my statement to the FBI. What did I miss?" He took the seat next to his mother and looked around in confusion as everyone started laughing.

Morgan relaxed into her seat. Exhaustion was slowing taking over as she sipped her coffee and enjoyed the easy banter around her. Paige asked about her life in DC and if she enjoyed living in a big city. Morgan could tell Paige was trying very hard to make up for the way she had previously treated her. The old Morgan would've held onto the grudge. As she sat there with laughter around her and Miles's arm around her shoulder, she decided it was time to let go of the past. She felt the anger and the bitterness slide away and decided from here on out she was going to focus on the happiness of the future.

"Morgan?" Pam drew her attention away from her thoughts and back to the present. "Can I join you?"

Morgan looked at her normally composed sister and saw nervousness in her eyes along with sadness. They had been best friends until Morgan started to look like her biological father, which caused their parents to break their sisterly bond. "Of course you can." Morgan smiled and saw Pam's face transform into guarded happiness.

"John called me this morning and told me all about what happened last night. Are you alright?" Pam asked as she took the last empty seat at the table.

"I am. Thank you, Pam." Morgan smiled at her sister and wished they could be close once again. She was so tired of feeling alone. She had been observing the Davies family and a desire hit her like she'd never had before—a desire to have children, to see them playing with their cousins while she and Pam laughed at their games. Miles appeared and laughed along with them. She wanted that more than anything else in the world.

"Then I heard what Miss Lily said about you working with the FBI to do what was right." Pam leaned forward and dropped her voice so that their conversation was private. "It got me thinking. A person who would risk their life for people she didn't even know would have an innate sense of right and wrong." Morgan nodded, but wondered where her sister was going with this. Pam nibbled on her lower lip, just like Morgan did when she was thinking before continuing, "You didn't really kiss Stephen did you?"

"No. I was asleep and woke to find his hands on me," Morgan said a little more harshly than she intended.

Pam shook her head, the sadness coming back into her eyes. "Why didn't you say anything?"

"I tried to, but Dad was already blaming me and kicking me out of the house. And then Stephen was telling you all that I was seducing him. No one would've believed me, so why bother?" Morgan shrugged and tried to pretend the accusations no longer stung.

"I'm so sorry Morgan. I made your life miserable. No wonder you never came back." Tears glistened in Pam's eyes as she pulled out a tissue from the pocket of her navy blue, perfectly creased slacks.

"It's okay, Pam. It was a long time ago," Morgan said, realizing that she no longer felt the anger she once held for her sister. She felt so free now. Free to love, free to move on with her life.

"No, it's not. I was horrible and Dad just encouraged it. Why would he do that?" Pam asked a little too loud for Morgan's taste.

Miles turned his head toward them now and the rest of the table did a poor job of pretending not to listen. Well, if Morgan was to move forward she needed to tell them all the truth. Her mother had tried to find the courage after she left, but couldn't. Morgan may be beaten and bruised, but she had courage in spades.

"He did it because I wasn't his child and he hated me for it." Pam's eyes went large and her hand covered her open mouth. Morgan heard the sharp intake of breath that came from the table, but then she felt the reassuring feel of Miles's hand on her shoulder. "Mom told me the afternoon of my disownment. She fell in love with a man in Cincinnati. She found out she was pregnant and was about to leave Dad when she got a call telling her that her lover had died. Dad threatened her with social abandonment and disgrace if she left. So she made a deal with him to claim me as his in return for her staying and not causing him any embarrassment either at being cuckolded."

Pam closed her eyes while she processed what she had just heard. Her lips began to quiver as tears rolled down her cheeks. She took the offered napkins and wiped tears away before reaching for Morgan's hand. "No wonder you didn't come back to his funeral. It was you that left roses at Mom's grave every year, wasn't it?"

"Yes. I was at the funeral too. Mom and I talked every Saturday for two hours until she passed."

"I feel as if everything I've known has been a lie," Pam whispered as her tears began again. She took a deep breath and pulled herself together, squaring her shoulders as she looked anew at the sister she willingly pushed away. With a big grin she said, "The only thing for certain is that we have so much to catch up on! I have to get my kids. They always wanted to have an aunt. Do you mind? I'll get them out of school so they can spend the whole day with you. Wait, first I'll go tell Jeffery and then we'll get the kids. Oh Morgan, this is going to be wonderful!" Pam threw her arms around Morgan and pulled her into a tight hug.

"Oh that's so sweet!" Paige dabbed her eyes and then pinned her brother with a stare. "Miles, I want a sister. You guys never do that."

Morgan looked up and found Miles looking at her with such adoration that she felt her heart melt. She longed to leap into his arms and kiss him.

"I'll do my best, sis."

"I have to go get Jeffery and then the kids. I'll meet you back here in thirty minutes." Pam hurried out the front door with a large smile on her face. Morgan looked around and found Miss Daisy and Miss Violet with their heads together, tears in their eyes and smiles on their faces.

"Someone needs an order of pecan pancakes," Miss Violet sniffled as she disappeared into the kitchen.

Chapter Twenty-One

Miles leaned back in his chair and rested his arm around Morgan's shoulders. He absently traced a circle with his thumb over the borrowed Kentucky sweatshirt and found himself thinking about running his hands over her soft skin instead of the shirt. He smiled as she laughed at a story his mother was telling her. If he had actually been paying attention instead of daydreaming about ripping off her clothes, then he probably would've been embarrassed. His mother loved to tell childhood stories about him. Her favorites were the stories of the serious elder brother who liked orders, schedules, and sometimes wore a superman cape when he was doing his chores.

Morgan laughed again and placed her hand on his knee as she looked up at him. God, he loved this woman. There were no if, ands, or buts about it. The feeling was bursting up from his heart and he knew he never wanted to spend another day away from her. If he weren't in a room full of people he would tell her how much she had come to mean to him.

Miles glanced around the café. The mismatched tables and chairs were mostly empty now. Miss Daisy was arranging the small vases of flowers on the tables while Miss Violet was humming as she flipped pancakes. Miles found himself smiling. He was happy. He realized the feelings he had so long shoved aside as he was busy making the grades in college, serving his country, and building his company, just made him smile even more.

"Knock it off Cole!" Paige smacked her husband as she and the rest of the table laughed. "I swear, he's actually very nice when he's not in cop mode. And, this will make you like him—he ticks off Kandi faster than anyone I know. Do you remember her?"

"Oh my gosh! Is there anyone in a ten-year span that wasn't tormented by her? She was younger than me, but she still managed to plague me daily. Well then Agent Parker, maybe you've risen some in my esteem," Morgan joked as Miss Violet set a plate of pecan pancakes in front of each of them.

"Why thank you, ma'am." Cole took a bow in his seat with a flourish of his hand. The pancakes in front of him exploded. Pieces of delicious pancake covered his face.

"What in tarnation?" Miss Violet leaned over the plate of pancakes to get a better look, "Someone shot my pancakes!"

Cole, Miles, Pierce and Jake whipped their heads around to the front window. Miles cursed as they saw a man dressed in black racing toward them from across the street with a gun in his hand. He had to have been hiding behind a parked car when he took the shot at Cole. After missing he went all in.

As Miles reached for Morgan, Cole was already grabbing Paige. Pierce leaned over and grabbed Miss Violet as their father lunged in front of their mother. Pulling and pushing simultaneously, everyone went crashing to the floor as the back of Cole's chair splintered with a direct hit.

"What the hell happened?" Miles heard Morgan mumble from where her face was smashed against the floor. He was sprawled completely over her, protecting her from the onslaught. His large body on top of hers made it hard for her to breathe.

"We're being shot at!" Miles told her as he looked around to make sure no one had been hit. The rest of the diners were under their tables except for Miss Lily's old neighbor, Edna, who was digging around in her purse.

"Sorry about that Miss Violet," Pierce said as he smiled down at Miss Violet sprawled on the floor. Her ever-present spatula was still in her hand.

"Oh, don't be sorry, dear. Y'all may want to go out the back door."

Miles vaulted up, pulling Morgan with him. Bullets shattered the window as the man walked calmly toward them firing. "Run low to the ground, quickly!"

Cole pulled his gun from his holster, "Pierce, take care of your sister!" He aimed his weapon and fired off some shots causing the man to lunge back behind a parked car across the street from the café.

Jake was already pushing Marcy out the back door as Miles and Morgan reached the kitchen. Miles, Morgan, Pierce, and Paige slammed through the back door seconds behind his parents. No one spoke until the door flew open and Cole burst out.

"Oh thank God!" Paige flung her arms around her husband. "What was that all about? Why are we being shot at?"

"It doesn't make sense. That was William Brady, Top Producers' head of security. He should be shooting at me, not you," Morgan said as she tried to steady her breath.

"No, it does make sense. They must've been watching us because they shot at me—the one with all the evidence in his pocket," Cole said as he patted the flash drive containing the proof needed to bring Top Producers and David Washington down.

"What do we do now?" Marcy asked.

"He wants us, not you all. Cole, Morgan, and I are all that matter to him. We need to split up." Miles felt the familiar hardness come over him as if it were a second skin. This wasn't the Middle East mountains, this was his hometown and he definitely had home-court advantage. "How many guns do you have?" Miles asked Cole before explaining his plan.

"Only this one, sorry." Cole pulled out second magazine and shoved it into place.

"It's okay, I don't need one." And he didn't. He'd done a lot worse than take out a single armed man with nothing but his hands. "We'll go around the side of the building and then split. Mom—you, Dad, Pierce, and Paige run behind these buildings and hide. I'll go with Morgan to the right." Miles laid out his plan as he did to his troops, only this time his heart was involved.

"If you provide a distraction, I can get across the street. I should be able to get a clear shot off if I can flank him. I'm sure Noodle and Dinky will be here any second now." Cole nodded toward the small alley on the far side of the café. "I can come out there and surprise him."

"Wait." Marcy held up her hands. "You're going to use Miles and Morgan as *bait*?"

"That's exactly what we're going to do." Miles turned to his mother and saw that her face had managed to go another shade whiter.

"No. I won't allow it," her voice quivered as tears sprang to her eyes.

"It's okay Mrs. Davies. This is my mess. I'll do it alone. You all get to safety. Please," Morgan begged. She looked at him and Miles felt a whole other level of hardness he had never known come over him. He knew without a doubt he would die for this woman and there was no way he'd let harm come to her. The resolve he had in battle was nothing to what he was feeling now.

"No. You'll go and I'll be your cover. Everyone, move now!" Miles grabbed Morgan's hand and dragged her toward the side street as he watched Cole sprint toward the small alley. "Make sure you give me a couple of minutes, no more than three!" Miles just nodded to Cole as he headed for the street.

"Miles! Please. I can't let you do this. I would die if anything happened to you. I love you too much. Please, let me do this alone!" Morgan pleaded as they turned up the street and ran toward Main Street.

"I still think there's something you don't understand and that may be my fault for not telling you. See, I thought you had ruined my life when I got that phone call from you. And you have. You've ruined the isolated life I had set up for myself. You've ruined the daily routine I established and you've ruined my ability to think of anything but you. You consume my mind when you're not with me and drive me wild when you are. I love you with all my heart and soul and there's no way I'll ever let anything happen to you." Miles slowed to a stop and looked around the corner. William Brady was looking through the shattered window of the café trying to find them.

"You love me?" Miles heard Morgan whisper.

"Sweetheart, I'd move heaven and earth to be with you. Now, zigzag to the first building and duck in the doorway."

"Miles! Really? Now you're saying all this?" Morgan rolled her eyes as she felt her heart swell. Miles smiled down at her. He'd do more than just tell her how much she meant to him, he'd show her every day for the rest of their lives that he would give his life for her in a heartbeat.

"Yep. Get ready." He pulled her toward him, her back fitting tight against his chest. "Run, Morgan!" Miles screamed loud enough to draw the attention of Brady. Morgan took off at a run. She kept bent over, making herself as small as possible and as she ran diagonals across the street.

Miles kept one hand on her waist as he moved with her, blocking any bullets that might be fired at them. He didn't have to wait long. The first one pinged off the pavement just a foot from them. Miles heard the sound of shell cartridges bouncing off the sidewalk as the man emptied his clip.

Miles could tell from his erratic firing that Brady was getting mad. Good. When emotions bubbled up to the surface they knocked your aim off. Morgan was still running with her arms over her head, so he pushed slightly on her waist to direct her to dive into the doorway of Keeneston Antiques and Knickknacks. Morgan responded instantly, slamming into the closed glass door of the shop.

"What's going on?" Morgan gasped between gulps of air.

Miles looked around the corner and spotted Brady, gun raised, walking toward them. His hair was slicked back and he was in full combat gear. "Stay back. He's coming this way." Miles looked toward the alley for Cole when two white heads and one steel gray head drew his attention. Miss Violet stood in the window with a heavy pot in her hand. Miss Daisy and Edna peaked out from each side of Violet's plump frame.

"Oh no," Miles moaned as he watched a pot come flying out the broken window right at Brady. He tensed, ready to run right at the man if he turned on the women. The pot hit Brady right in the middle of the back sending Brady stumbling forward. Before he could recover another pot was hurled from the window, hitting him on the shoulder. The three heads ducked back inside the café before Brady could turn around.

Miles searched for Cole, but before he could see him, another white head teetered across the street with a large broom in hand. At least Miss Lily had crossed the street a good two blocks away so she wasn't overly obvious, but he knew instantly what she meant to do with that broom. "Come on Cole," he whispered as a frying pan arched through the air.

Brady had had enough and fired off two warning shots into the café and then turned and fired a couple toward Miles. The bullets hit the brick and lodged in the old mortar.

"He shot at us!" Miles heard Miss Violet scream in anger.

"Miles, is that Miss Violet?" Morgan whispered as she tried to get a closer look. Miles pushed her back to make sure she was completely protected from the gunman.

"Bless his heart, he couldn't hit the broad side of a barn with aim like that!" Miss Daisy said, rather loudly, back to her sister. These women were going to be the death of Miles. He just knew it.

"Ain't that the truth?" Apparently Miss Lily had made it successfully into the café, Miles thought.

"Move over! I got this!" another voice rang out down the quiet Main Street.

"Miles, who was that?" Morgan whispered, trying again to push her way to look out.

"That would be your everyday gun-toting granny, Edna." Miles looked back around the corner and saw that the elderly women had Brady confused. He kept looking where Miles and Morgan were, trying to decide if he should advance further, or take out the white-haired, pot-throwing mafia.

Brady decided against the women in the café and walked toward Miles and Morgan as he continued to pull the trigger in steady succession. Miles stepped fully in front of Morgan and prepared for hand-to-hand combat.

As Miles tensed for attack, the sound of a second gun shook the earth. It sounded as if a cannon had gone off. He felt it in his feet as the heavy noise reverberated up the street. Miles looked around the corner to see little Edna with the long barrel of a 500 Smith and Wesson Magnum propped up in the window of the café. Miss Daisy and Miss Violet were each bracing Edna against the power of the gun as Miss Lily was in turn bracing her sisters.

Brady looked shocked. He was frozen in place as he stared at the women. Miles didn't hesitate as he sprang from behind the wall and sprinted full speed into Brady. They crashed to the ground, Miles grappled with Brady as they both tried to reach the dropped gun. They rolled and Miles stood up, dragging Brady with him by his collar.

Miles landed a solid punch and saw Brady's head snap back. But Brady wasn't out yet. Miles was advancing on him when Brady lashed out with a kick to his midsection. Miles exhaled on the kick and felt a rib crack, but it wasn't enough to bring him down. Not when he was protecting the woman he loved.

"That's enough!" The time it took to recover from the kick was enough for Brady to grab his secondary weapon from behind his back. Miles growled as he studied the best angle for attack. "You try it and I shoot her." Brady shifted his gun to point directly at Morgan who had come around the side of the wall. Miles held up his hands and took some big steps backward trying to get in position to protect Morgan from a shot.

With tires squealing from behind, Miles jumped back to block Brady's shot as he watched Morgan scramble behind the wall. Now that Morgan was safe, he ran as fast as he could away from Brady, as a silver minivan sped toward them. It flew by him, too fast for Miles to see who was driving. All he could see were four white stick-figure stickers and a Dale Jr. sticker as it roared by him.

Miles turned back around just in time to see the driver steer toward a shocked Brady. With his mouth and eyes wide open, the minivan hit him. Brady was launched high into the air. He landed on top of the minivan and bounced a couple of times before the vehicle slid to a stop. Brady was trying to anchor himself to the hood, but the momentum was too much. He couldn't hold onto anything and went sailing through the air, landing on the ground with a grunt. The door opened and Pam Gilbert stepped out of the minivan.

Morgan raced to Miles's side. "Holy crap! Your sister just ran Brady over," Miles said in amazement as he wrapped Morgan in a fierce hug.

"Well bless her heart."

William Brady opened his eyes slowly. The world was out of focus, but seemed very bright. The last thing he remembered was a minivan barreling toward him. He blinked his eyes until the blurriness focused into four little white heads. It was those damn women! He must have died and gone to Hell. One was holding a wooden spoon, one a spatula, another a broom, and the last one held a very large Smith and Wesson Magnum pointed right at his head.

"You just got run over by a soccer mom—bet that hurts worse than knowing you're going to jail," the one with the broom laughed.

"Did you see him flying through the air?" the one with wooden spoon chuckled.

"Real tough guy, that one," the woman with the spatula laughed.

"You made my day, punk" the lady with the gray hair said as the targeted FBI agent stepped into his view wearing a huge smile, surrounded by sheriff deputies.

"Mr. Brady, the FBI is requesting your presence at our office for a nice long chat. Let me introduce myself. I'm Special Agent in Charge, Cole Parker, and you're under arrest."

Chapter Twenty-Two

Morgan stood with her mouth shaped into a perfect O as her sister jumped out of the minivan, now with a considerable dent on the roof, and walked over to William with her hands on her hips. It was over, it was all over and everyone was okay! Relief flooded her as she realized the end was finally in sight.

She felt Miles close the space between them as he wrapped his strong arms around her and pulled her to his chest. "I love you," he whispered before bringing his lips to hers. She forgot about Pam, the herd of elderly women, and the flock of law enforcers. All she could think about was the feel of Miles's hard body against hers. The taste of his mouth on hers was much more interesting than what would happen to William Brady.

"Hmm. I love you too," Morgan whispered as she pulled away from him. His eyes were burning with a vibrancy that told her exactly what he was thinking.

"Morgan! Oh, thank God!" Pam screeched as she rushed toward her. The passenger door to the minivan opened and a very wide-eyed man got out. She recognized Pam's husband, Jeffery, from the café. The poor man looked like he was going to pass out.

Pam hit her at full speed, pushing Miles out of the way as she crushed Morgan in a fierce hug. "I had just picked up Jeffery when I heard some loud noise. I thought it was an explosion. I hurried downtown to see that man standing in the middle of the street with a gun!" Pam rushed on, hardly taking a breath. "And then he was firing the gun and I saw Miles covering you and I didn't know what to do!" Pam started to sob, causing her perfectly done makeup to smear and run down her face. "I just found you and I wasn't going to lose you. I just floored it! Oh and then he actually hit the car! Did you see him bounce? He got some good air as my kids would say. And poor Jeffery, he hasn't said a word since and now my minivan's roof is caved in, although I had really been hoping for a new one for my birthday—you know, the ones with the built in DVD players and the storage space beneath the seat—but I don't know if insurance will cover this. What do you think?"

"Pammy Cakes, I'll buy you the top-of-the-line model with leather seats and all if you promise me that you'll never run over another person. I don't think I could take that again!" Average Jeffery exhaled and some color returned to his cheeks.

"Oh, Jeffy! I'm so sorry I scared you. I love you baby!" Pam ran into her husband's arm and planted a huge kiss on him right there in the middle of Main Street. Morgan was willing to bet that was the least average thing Pam had ever done. Well, that and bouncing a guy off her minivan.

Morgan smiled. At least she had expanded her sister's horizons. And a sister who would send a guy sailing off her car was one she wanted to get to know better. Miles saw her smile and slipped his arm around her. Morgan snuggled her head against his chest and knew her life was never going to be the same again.

"Oh! Morgan!" Pam broke from her kiss and introduced her very dazed husband to her. "Jeffery, this is my sister. She'll be joining us tonight for dinner with the kids. Miles, you know where we live. See you at six. We have to go buy a new minivan!" Pam gave her a wink and dragged her husband away.

"There's something else I'd rather do tonight, but I guess it can wait until after dinner," Miles whispered as his lips tickled the soft skin behind her ear. "It'll have to wait, though—incoming."

Morgan opened her eyes to see that the town had lost interest in William and was now heading straight for her. She tried to back up, but Miles held her in place with a wicked grin on his face. "Time to pay the piper, sweetheart."

Morgan was lost in a sea of white hair, brown uniforms, and enough people talking to make her head spin. People hugged her, asked questions, and decided if she was to be forgiven or not. Finally, Miss Lily thumped her broom against the pavement to get everyone's attention.

"I just have one question. Is there anything else you did that we need to know about?"

"I was the one who painted the water tower, not Miles."

"You painted the water tower?" Miss Lily gasped.

"I told you," Mr. Wolfe said from the safety of the other side of the group.

"I did. And I tipped the cows at Mr. Johnson's farm, I broke your mailbox Miss Edna, and I stole gum from the market all to get my daddy's attention. It was wrong and I apologize to all of you," Morgan said with great sincerity.

"What about turning the cheerleaders blue?" someone asked from the crowd.

"Yeah, not so sorry about that one," Morgan laughed and at her apology the town seemed to begin to thaw toward her. She knew it was just the beginning, though. She'd need to earn their trust and respect over time.

Morgan opened the door to her hotel and Bill sauntered through it, his belly hanging low after all the food he had snuck from Marcy's table. After giving their statements to the horde of FBI agents, Marcy had herded them to her farm and fed them.

"Come on, Bill. Let's get a nice bed for you." Morgan walked over to the closet and pulled out a large pillow and an extra thick blanket. She laid it on the far side of the room and smiled down as Bill curled up and fell asleep instantly.

Could this be her life now: a snoring dog, a handsome man who loved her, a sister, and a family? The town was learning to accept her. She even had found a friend in Annie, and all the other women had made an effort to talk to her tonight. Morgan could hardly imagine a life where she had love, family, and friends.

"What are you thinking about, sweetheart?" Miles asked as he unbuttoned his shirt, revealing the hard lines of his chest.

"You. Me. Us." Morgan kicked off her shoes and stepped toward Miles.

"That sounds serious. What about us?" Miles slid the shirt off his well-defined arms and laid it on one of the chairs. She tried not to stare, but she suddenly felt very, very hot.

"I was thinking about maybe not rushing back to DC. What do you think?" Morgan asked hesitantly.

"I think that sounds like a wonderful idea, and let me show you all the reasons why." Miles sat down on the bed and pulled her toward him. He wrapped his hands around her hips moving her between his legs. His hands practically burned through her clothes.

"You look flushed, let's get you out of those clothes." Miles slid his hands up her ribcage, brushing the sides of her breasts as he pulled her shirt off. Yes, staying in Keeneston would have some very nice benefits indeed.

Afghanistan, six years ago…

Miles felt the familiar dream start up again, but he was helpless to wake himself. He was shoving a bleeding and unconscious Cade into the sedan and grabbing the keys to find out who was banging inside the trunk.

He reached out slowly with the keys in his hands. He had calmed his breathing and was ready for whatever he found in the trunk. With his gun in the other hand he slowly inserted the key. With a slow and deliberate twist of the key Miles felt the lock give. He raised his gun and stepped back to watch as the trunk popped open.

A blonde woman stared at him with wide eyes as she pushed herself farther back into the trunk. She had been beaten badly. Her face was swollen and black and blue. Her lip was split and there was dried blood coming from her nose. Miles knew she would be screaming if it hadn't been for the dirty cloth stuck in her mouth.

"Mariah? Mariah Brown?" he asked in a soft, yet authoritative tone. The woman stilled and then nodded frantically. "I'm Captain Miles Davies with the United States Delta Force. I've come to rescue you. I'm going to pull out a knife now and cut your bindings, okay?"

When she nodded again he reached into the trunk and cut the rope digging into her ankles and wrists. She quickly reached for her mouth and yanked out the rag. He scanned the area as he held out his hand to assist her out of the trunk. She was just a child, about Paige's age and it pained him to think of someone like her going through this.

"Thank you! Thank you so much Captain Davies." Mariah sobbed as she climbed out of the trunk and collapsed into his arms.

"Are you injured?"

"No, just relieved. I'm sorry, my legs aren't doing too good of a job holding me up right now. I've been in that trunk for God knows how long."

"I'm sorry, but you're not going to have time to stretch them now. My brother is in the car injured and we need to get to safety." He took out his compass and field map and started to devise a plan.

"Oh my God! You're injured! Let me look at it. I took first aid when I was a lifeguard." Mariah grabbed his brown camouflage before he could stop her.

"It's okay ma'am. I'm fine. It's more important we get out of here quickly." Miles looked down at the map again. "We were supposed to hike back into the mountains and cross the border back into Tajikistan. Although we have troops on the ground in Afghanistan, this mountainous part of the country is still ruled by rebel factions.

Farkhor Air Force Base is the closest to us. The trouble is there's only one road into Darvaz and there's a large bridge we'd have to cross."

"What's the problem with that?" Mariah asked.

"The problem is when your kidnappers discover you're gone, they'll be looking for us on that road and that bridge is the first place they'll set up."

Miles stepped away from Mariah and pulled out his satellite phone. "Major, it's Alpha One. I have the package, but we need a new exit. Alpha Two is injured and no longer mobile. What are my new orders?"

Miles nodded as he listened to the voice on the other end of the phone. He gave a quick summary of the surrounding area, the manpower he had seen, and the fact that he had a car. "Yes, sir. We'll meet Bravo team in eight hours. Alpha One out."

Miles found Mariah staring at him when he turned around. "We're going deeper into the mountains. There's a goat trail that's big enough for the car, but not much else. There's a good chance we won't be able to make it the whole way, but we can get horses there."

"Why can't they pick us up here?"

"The area is way too hot. The drone picked up rebels coming this way. They're about 30 minutes away. There isn't enough time for our guys to get here and the rebels are known to have ground to air missiles in the mountains. We have to move now."

Mariah nodded and hurried to the passenger door. Miles checked on Cade and was relieved to see that he was still breathing strong and steadily even though he remained unconscious.

"Where are we going?" Mariah asked as she looked nervously around.

"We're trying to make it to a small mountain village called Vanj. We'll follow this small road, if you can even call it that, through the mountains and then turn north on the road traveling along the border until we can go farther west into Tajikistan. It should take seven to eight hours for an exit group to meet us with a medevac chopper."

"Then let's get going. I can't tell you how badly I want to be home." Mariah shivered and rubbed her arms to warm herself. She hopped into the car and gave Miles a couple of minutes to use his field kit to clean the wound and pour some quick clotting granules on the gunshot wound. He gritted his teeth as the granules burned in the wound.

Miles lowered his shirt and took all evidence of blood and bandages and tossed them in the trunk. Mariah was quiet as he drove away from the rescue scene. He drove for five minutes as fast as he could before turning around and driving the other direction. He drove in a large circle covering a couple of miles hoping the tire marks would be too confusing to follow before heading in their true direction.

They were almost to the border when he realized Mariah hadn't said a word. He had been concentrating on handling the car. It was made for off-road racing and it ate up the dirt roads as it went into the mountains. However, the roads turned to rock as they wound through the mountains toward the border.

"Are you sure you're alright?" Miles asked as he took a tight corner. "I know we're on a tight schedule ma'am, but let me know if you need anything."

"Thank you, Captain. I'm alright besides being banged around some. I dare say my face and ribs will heal. Now, if I'll ever be able to forget about this, I don't know, but I pray I do. Do you want me to check on your brother? He was injured saving me, wasn't he?"

"Yes, ma'am, he was. I'd appreciate it if you checked his pulse and breathing. I'm pretty sure he has slipped into a coma. I just hope the swelling in his brain goes down soon and he wakes up. I'll get you both to a hospital by tomorrow morning."

Miles slowed the car as he took a sharp turn. He was only thirty minutes from the border by his calculations, however it would be another two hours until he reached their evacuation point. He was ahead of schedule now, but he wasn't about to slow down and give the rebels a chance to catch up to them.

"Do you know why they took you?"

"Yes. As you know, my father is Secretary of State. We're really close and he tells me probably more than he should," Mariah paused and grinned slightly at the memory of her father before starting again. "He was negotiating behind the scenes with several major players in the Middle East, Europe, and Asia to orchestrate a no-fly zone and completely sever monetary and humanitarian aid to the area I was in. It was going to be a first… denying help to specific sections of the region spanning multiple countries without blocking any entire nation."

"How could your father get Pakistan and Afghanistan to agree to this?" Miles couldn't believe her father could accomplish such a feat.

"He threatened to completely blockade the countries of all aid and financial support from the United States," Mariah said as she turned around and put her fingers to Cade's neck.

"That would never fly. The US depends on oil exports. I can't see the President agreeing to it."

"Privately, the President put out that he would back it. It was a bluff, but it worked. It worked so well that the rebels who call these mountains home, kidnapped me. The ransom was a UN Treaty saying US supports the current regimes and, in return for their cooperation during this War on Terror, would never place sanctions on them. In fact the treaty would call for an increase in aid with no restrictions. The US would avoid the black eye of having the Secretary of State's own daughter kidnapped and then murdered.

"They were transporting me to an allied country. The plan was to kill me there and force the US to spread the War of Terror to a third front, thus spreading out our troops. I don't know which country they were planning to frame; I'm guessing Iran or Saudi Arabia since those are two of the top-producing oil companies in tension with the US's War on Terror. They'd be blamed and then the US would either attack to save face, or put forth tough sanctions that would harm them through denial of oil sales."

"I see. Either way the heat would be off this area." Miles nodded as the vehicle started down the side of the mountain.

"Yes, exactly." Mariah turned around from the backseat, "Your brother's fine. He's not responding when I pinch him, but his breathing is strong and steady."

"Thank you. I'm…" Miles slammed on his brakes as he rounded a corner. The road was already one lane, but the side of it was crumbling from water runoff. He slowed down and pulled as close to the mountainside as he could.

"Look out!" Mariah screamed and pointed down the road.

Miles cursed and slammed on his brakes. Ahead of him were five men blocking the road with machine guns. He threw the car into reverse and looked into the review mirror to find five more men blocking the road. They were trapped.

"Captain, those are the men that kidnapped me!"

"How do you know?"

"Their robes, they all had red, green and black trim along the bottom. Those were their colors."

Mariah was panicked. He looked at all the men and sure enough they all had the same casual uniform on. He could try to back over them, but he wouldn't be able to hit them all and they had powerful guns. More and more men appeared from the mountain. When he saw the bazooka he knew they had no options. They were outnumbered and outgunned. He looked around and then down. Down might be the only way out.

"Mariah, we're trapped. We have two options. We surrender and hope for an escape in the future or…"

"I'll take the or."

"Okay, then hold on tight." Miles turned around and buckled Cade in the best he could before strapping on his seatbelt. "I'd buckle that if I were you." Miles didn't hesitate as he pressed on the gas and drove the car off the side of the mountain.

The runoff had created a path down the mountainside and he just hoped like hell it was clear. The car took to the air and landed head first on the path. Miles's head slammed against the roof of the car and he heard Mariah scream. He managed to keep his hands on the wheel and the car on the small path created over the seasons.

The car bounced and picked up speed as it headed down the hill. He pressed on the brakes only to find that the car would fishtail at such speeds and on such unstable ground. Mud, slush, and patches of rocks made navigating the car difficult. Ahead of him there was a drop-off. He couldn't see how big it was but they were about to find out.

He slammed on the brakes, the car fishtailed and went over the drop-off sideways, passenger side first. Miles gripped the steering wheel as if he could control the car mid-air. The car's hood dipped with the weight of the engine and hit the ground passenger headlight first. The airbag deployed a second before Miles's face slammed into the steering wheel. His head was knocked back with the force of the airbag, the impact crumpled the engine block causing it to collapse on his legs. He felt his right ankle snap right before the car came to rest.

The first thing that Miles noticed was the silence. He reached for his belt and unsheathed his knife. He plunged it into his airbag and filled his lungs with a huge breath when it deflated. Mariah's eyes were closed and there was fresh blood dripping down the side of her airbag. He similarly ripped into hers, causing it to deflate. Mariah's head slumped forward as he checked for a pulse. He let out a breath when he felt one.

Turning in his seat, he clenched his jaw against the pain in his leg to check on Cade. Cade had been thrown from his seat and was wedged on the floor. Shouting his name, Miles reached frantically for him. He couldn't reach his head, but managed to grab his hand. His pulse was still there, thank God.

Mariah moaned and Miles immediately went to her. "Mariah? Mariah? Wake up, dear. Come on, you can do it. Open your eyes."

"Am I dead Captain?"

"Not yet. Are you hurt badly?"

"I can't feel my leg."

Miles could hear the panic setting in and tried to calm her. "It's okay. Breathe, breathe deeply." He talked long enough to get her focused on her breathing. He had to get them out of here before those men found them—and they would if they didn't move.

Miles tried to pull his leg out, but his boot was stuck. He'd have to twist his whole leg in order to wiggle it out. Pain radiated through him and he broke out in a sweat as he forced himself to move. He grunted in pain as he pulled hard and fell out of his seat and onto the rocky ground.

He pulled up his pant leg and said a quick prayer of thanks when he took off his boot. The broken bone wasn't protruding, so he might be able to set it. He stood up and hobbled over to Mariah's door. When he opened it, he saw why she couldn't feel her leg. Everything below the knee was completely crushed by the car.

"Okay. This is going to take some work. Let me fix my ankle and then I'll get the crowbar out and pry you free. Keep taking deep breaths, okay?" Miles looked around and found two small boulders that he could use. These mountains were so barren there were no trees for making a splint.

He hobbled over to the rocks, put as little pressure as possible on his leg, and sat down. Miles wedged his boot between the boulders and took a deep breath. This was going to hurt. He pulled slightly until his ankle was in traction and then set the bone. He cried out in pain, but then sighed with relief. Now he needed to splint it, but he'd do that after he got Cade and Mariah taken care of.

Hopping on one leg, he found the crowbar in the trunk and went to work prying Mariah's leg from the wreckage. "I'm almost done. Can you feel your leg yet?"

"No. It's still numb, why? What does that mean?"

"It means you could be bleeding internally." Miles pulled off his belt and cinched it tight around her knee before pulling out the last piece of metal pinning her down. "Come on, let's get you out of here." Miles helped her from the car and propped her against the small boulders he'd used to set his ankle.

Next he had to check on his brother. Cade was breathing, but still in a coma. He had some new injuries from the wreck, but they all seemed to be superficial. Miles pulled him from the car with much less hassle than Mariah and laid him next to her. It was time to tear the car apart if they were going to get anywhere. He used his knife to cut the seatbelts out of the car and laid them out on the ground. Then he went to the trunk and took out the rope, emergency kit, and floor mat. He dug out two holes on the top of the mat using his knife and threaded the rope through them.

Miles pulled out his medical kit and used the tape to wrap around the ends of the rope, creating a place to grab without the rope slicing into his hands. Then he took his knife and cut four slits into the thick mat. He threaded two seat belts through them.

"What are you doing?" Mariah asked in complete confusion.

"Getting you and Cade transportation."

"I don't get it."

"You will soon. I just need to splint my ankle and then we'll be ready to move." Miles took the crowbar and placed it along his leg. He secured it as tight as he could against the side of his leg and ankle using medical tape.

"Captain! You're bleeding again." Mariah pointed to his side where the gunshot wound had gone through him in what seemed like a lifetime ago.

"It's not bad. We need to get moving." Miles grabbed Cade and awkwardly carried him to the mat. Laying him down he pulled the two ends of the center seatbelt over Cade, clicked them together, and pulled tight, securing Cade to the mat.

"Oh. But, how am I going to fit? There are no more seatbelts." Maria asked as she tried to help him get her to the mat.

"Sorry, but you're just going to have to hold on. Can you do that?"

"Yes, but do you really think you can drag us all the way to civilization?"

"I don't need civilization, I just need a horse." Miles helped Mariah down onto the mat and pulled out his satellite phone. Dammit. It was junk now. There was no other option. He had to get them to their rendezvous point by himself. Miles put each piece of rope over his shoulders and started down the mountain.

It had been the longest two hours of his life. He knew he had barely covered four miles when off in the distance he saw a river running through the valley. Hope soared. Where there was water, there was civilization.

Sure enough before he even made it to the grassy banks he saw a boy leading two trail horses. "Mariah, stay here and don't make a sound. I'm getting us some better transportation."

He spent every afghani he had to buy those horses and send the boy on his way with the story that the horses spooked and got away. He also negotiated three-minutes use of the kid's cell phone. He took the horses up the mountainside and stopped them where Mariah and Cade were hiding behind a jagged rock.

"You and I will ride this one and I'll put Cade on the other. The rendezvous point had been moved. We just need to get to the other side of the border. It'll take about two hours so hang on, we gotta move fast."

"Let's go, cowboy." Mariah grabbed a hold of his neck as he lifted her onto the horse. Miles tied Cade to the other horse with the rope and then mounted behind Mariah. The boy had told them they were around fifteen miles from the border. The terrain was flat in most parts, but they'd hit some rocky patches too, so they'd have to alternate between trotting and walking the horses.

Miles' ankle throbbed as he kept a tight grip on both Mariah and the reigns. She had grown very pale the last couple of miles. They were so close now, but the rebels had to be expecting them to be heading toward the border, unless they thought they were dead. But Miles doubted that. He was sure they would've found the car by now and followed the very clear trail that was left when he was dragging Mariah and Cade.

Up ahead he saw the marker for the border. He urged the horses into a gallop and kept an eye on the sky. The helicopter should be here any minute. He looked at his watch and felt a rush of adrenaline come over him. Four minutes until Bravo team arrived. He had never felt such relief as when he crossed over the border and into Tajikistan. His destination point was one mile in and he would be there right as the helicopter arrived.

Miles pushed the horses into a gallop as he heard the sound of the helicopter blades off in the distance. But his excitement died in an instant. He heard rebels yelling behind him. He turned and saw at least twenty men on horseback charging at him and closing fast.

Gunfire rang out as they fired at them. Mariah started praying as she held on for dear life. Miles unholstered his gun from his thigh and returned fire blindly over his shoulder as he urged their mounts forward.

Suddenly his horse screamed out and stumbled. He tried to urge the horse on, but it was useless, the horse was going to collapse and they'd be trapped when the animal fell on them. Pulling the horse to an immediate stop he jumped off, momentarily going blind as the white-hot pain shot through his leg when he hit the ground. He caught Mariah as the horse went down.

"Get on Cade's horse and ride as fast as you can while I hold them off!" He heaved her up and then handed her the rope used to guide the horse. He smacked the horse's flank and turned to lay down cover for them. As he took aim at the rebels he turned to see the helicopter approach. Cade and Mariah would make it.

Miles laid some more cover and when the clip emptied he turned and ran as fast as he could. His vision became blurry with the pain, but he managed to reload his gun and take a couple more shots as the helicopter came into firing position. Loud gunfire erupted from the helicopter as the pilot shot at the group of rebels.

"Captain!" Mariah shouted. "Look out!" She kicked her horse with her good leg and he knew she was coming toward him.

"Stay back!" he shouted.

Miles saw the group had split. Three men had gone wide and out of the helicopter's range as it tackled the larger group. The men raised their guns and Miles fired off every round he had. He took two of the men down by the time he ran out of bullets.

"Captain! Hop on!" Mariah yelled as she galloped toward him. The last man raised his gun and fired.

"No!" Miles roared as he leaped to protect Mariah, but it was too late. Mariah fell from the horse and lay motionless on the ground. Blood blossomed from under her and Miles knew he had failed her and himself.

Rage like he had never known overtook him. He was going to rip that bastard from limb to limb. He slid the magazine into his gun and turned to attack when a bullet slammed into his chest. He fell to the ground beside Mariah's body. His vision began to fade as he raised the gun and emptied his clip into the rebel.

Chapter Twenty-Three

"Miles! Miles, please wake up!" Morgan shook Miles as best as she could and cried into his ear. He had been flailing and mumbling in his sleep. She had woken up and found him drenched in sweat. She tried to wake him gently, but in a sudden movement he pushed her into the bed and threw himself on top of her.

"Miles. Please, you're getting heavy. I need you to wake up," Morgan pleaded, but he didn't move. He was still mumbling in his sleep and kept her pinned to the mattress. In her best boardroom voice she tried again. "Miles! Wake up now. Do you hear me? That's an order. Wake up right now!"

His head snapped up, "Mariah?"

"No, honey. It's me, Morgan. Are you okay?" Morgan gently cupped his face with her hands. His normally hard face was covered in sweat and so pale. When Morgan looked into his eyes she felt like crying at the pain she saw behind them.

Miles sat back on his knees and shook his head quickly trying to regain his composure. Bill whined and nudged Miles's arm before lying down beside him and resting his head on Miles's leg. Morgan watched as Miles ran his hand over his face and through his hair. She could tell that he wasn't quite sure what to do next.

"Miles, do you want to tell me what that was about?" she asked softly as she pulled the sheet up to cover her chest.

"Nothing. Just something that happened when I was overseas," Miles answered as he stared out the open hotel window.

"Miles? Who is Mariah?"

Miles snapped his head back to her, his eyes wide in surprise, "How do you know that name?" he accused.

"Calm down. You said her name in your sleep before and after you threw yourself on top of me."

"No one. Not anymore. Did I hurt you?"

"Of course not! But, don't change the subject, Miles. Who is Mariah?" Morgan watched as Miles battled his demons. She could tell that he couldn't decide whether or not to say anything more.

"She's the girl I killed," Miles said simply, yet the shimmer in his eyes told her the truth.

"I don't believe that for one second. Miles," Morgan took his hand in his and squeezed gently, "there's nothing that will stop me from loving you. I've been waiting a lifetime to be with you and someone as special as you deserves to be loved unconditionally. I need you to know that Miles. You're safe with me. You'll always be safe with me. Safe to tell me my cooking is bad, that I really do look fat in a dress, and that at night when you close your eyes your dreams are overtaken by darkness. Let me be your anchor. Let me be your light to chase away that darkness."

Miles got up from the bed and strode naked to the window to look out at the city lights illuminating the night sky. His muscles bunched under the invisible weight on his shoulders. Morgan worried about him and longed to go to him, but knew that this was something he had to do himself. She just needed to be there for him no matter what he said.

"I might not have pulled the trigger, but I killed her nonetheless and ever since then I've been paying the price for my failure," Miles spoke to the night. Morgan waited patiently for the reluctant story. "It was a rescue that went wrong. Cade was captured and beaten into a coma for three days. My target was Mariah Brown."

Morgan's eyes went wide. She knew the story of Mariah—everyone did. She was the college daughter of the former Secretary of State who was brutally murdered in Afghanistan after being kidnapped. It was such a powerful moment that led to the leveling of a whole mountain region known for harboring terrorists in a part of Afghanistan that bordered Pakistan and Tajikistan. But, in all the news coverage there was never any mention of a rescue.

"Cade and I took out a lot of the rebels before he was caught. I lost it. I allowed the rage to take me when I saw the gun to his head and I took them all out. That's when I found Mariah bloodied in the trunk of a car. We were tracked and attacked on a mountain pass close to the Tajikistan border. There were injuries to everyone, but I managed to get us to the border.

"A rescue copter was there and she was almost to safety when she turned back to try to save me from the last rebel. He killed her. She died in my arms and now she returns every night to my dreams to remind me I let an innocent kid die. I'll never forget her face." Miles paused and Morgan heard him swallow hard. "She smiled up at me and said, 'thank you.' And then she was gone."

Morgan stared at his wide back as it silently shook in the moonlight. The wounds from the knife were only physical and had healed long ago. His unhealed wounds were hidden. Hidden from the world and even hidden from him. "Miles, I don't think you'll believe what I'm going to say, but I don't think Mariah felt as if you failed her. She knew that and now it's time for you to know that."

"I can't do it. She reminded me so much of Paige. The whole time I kept thinking I had killed someone's little sister."

"But you didn't kill her. You have to learn to accept that. I can't make it better, but what I can do is tell you that I think what you did was heroic and I love you all the more because you're man enough to feel responsible for her. You did everything in your power to save her and for that, she was grateful. I'll also tell you that I think you need to channel these feelings into something besides guilt. Let me help you find a way. Miles..."

She held out her hand and waited for him to accept help. Morgan felt her arm trembling. She could only pray that he'd turn around to accept her help and all the love she could give him. Miles slowly circled and looked at her. Her breath caught as she waited for him to decide if he wanted to stay in the past or move with her into the future.

Miles raised his eyes and looked into the amethyst depths that were watching him. He had never told anyone what happened that night. He didn't know what had compelled him to tell her other than the overwhelming feeling of love they shared. He almost laughed as he thought how much his life had changed since this raven-haired vixen reentered it.

"Morgan, there's something I want you to do."

"Anything." She was so sincere. All he wanted to do was lose himself in her body for the rest of his life.

"Remind me to call Cade in the morning." Miles chuckled as her eyebrows shot up and her eyes widened. It wasn't what she had been expecting. But then she scrunched her nose and narrowed those gorgeous eyes at him for laughing at her. "To get the name of the PTSD specialist he saw."

"Oh Miles!" Morgan dropped the sheet and scrambled out of bed and straight into his arms.

"This is where I want you. You're my best medicine, sweetheart."

Miles raised her chin and placed his lips on hers. He gently rubbed his lips against hers teasing them both before sliding his tongue along the seam of her lips. He drew in her lower lip and nipped it gently as Morgan writhed against him trying to urge him for more.

"Patience, sweetheart. We have all the time in the world." He trailed his lips down her neck, over her collarbone, and to the hollow of her throat.

The throaty purrs that Morgan made just urged him on as she moved beneath his lips. Miles smiled against her breast as he teased her until she was panting with a need to match his own.

"Let me show you where I want you tonight," Morgan said breathlessly as she pulled him toward the bed.

"Yes, ma'am." Miles grinned and let his nurse take away the years of hurt.

Morgan and Miles laughed as they sat on the bed with trays of food on their laps. They had gotten up early that morning, made love, and decided they should probably have breakfast before it was time to head back into the real world. Her hotel room had served as a wonderful escape from the craziness of the day before. Morgan grinned as she pinched off a small piece of buttered biscuit. It had been the perfect night. She just wished it didn't have to end.

A knock at the door elicited a groan from both of them. "I fear our sanctuary is about to be interrupted," Miles said as he slid off the bed and tied the belt to the white hotel robe he was wearing.

Morgan leaned forward to see who had found them. Cole strode into the room wearing his black cowboy hat. "Sorry to interrupt. I thought you'd want an update."

This grabbed Morgan's attention. She had been worried he was there to interrogate her more. Although he was a nice guy, he wasn't so nice when she was on the receiving end of his questions. "What's going on, Agent Parker?" Morgan set aside her tray and swung her legs over the side of the bed.

"I think after all of this you better start calling me Cole or I might get my feelings hurt." Cole swept off his hat and took a little bow.

Morgan laughed at his antics, but then remembered why he was here. "What happened?"

"I got a call from Agent Salmonds. David Washington has been arrested in DC. He was caught at the airport trying to board a plane for Indonesia, which just happens to not have an extradition treaty with the US," Cole said as he leaned against the window.

"What does this mean for the future?" Morgan asked Cole.

"Well, for one, Top Producers is now being investigated by every government agency known to man. So, you probably don't have a job anymore."

"I think I can live with that," Morgan grinned.

"Now that it seems you have some time on your hands, maybe it's time to come home and clean up the mistakes from the past in order to move on to your future." Cole looked at Morgan and she thought he could see through her. Then he slowly looked over to Miles and put his hat back on. "Y'all have a good morning."

Cole stepped out the door and Morgan was left thinking about what he had said. She had thought about staying for a little while, but should she stay longer than that? Could she mend the fences she had broken down as a teenager and more importantly did she want to?

Chapter Twenty-Four

Two months later…

Morgan leaned against the hood of her car and basked in the warm May sun, enjoying that it was not blocked by large buildings. She leaned her head back and let her face soak up the rays as she waited for Miles. Just last month she and Miles had traveled to DC. together for her deposition in the David Washington hearing.

Miles had stayed by her side the whole time. When she was finished with her deposition, she had taken him around DC and showed him what her life would've been like had they not been living out of her hotel room while his house was being repaired.

The next day Miles had shown her his side of DC. They visited his old commanders and she listened as they swapped stories from training camp to missions. Then he took her to Walter Reed National Military Medical Center where they visited with some recovering troops Miles had met in Germany over Christmas.

Morgan had been so proud watching him talking with soldiers who seemed so alone in the huge complex. She could see him as the born leader he was when he stopped to talk to a private who was recovering from losing his leg in a roadside bombing. The kid had a case of hero worship when Miles revealed his name and rank. Miles ended up talking to him for an hour. They talked about their tours, their families, and the kid got misty-eyed when talking about missing his beloved dog at home. It was then Miles had gotten that determined look in his eye.

Morgan heard a door open and opened her eyes. People and dogs streamed out of the double glass doors. She caught sight of Miles with Bill trotting happily by his side as man and dog made their way toward her.

"How'd you boys do?" Morgan asked.

"We aced it. Bill is now a registered therapy dog!" Miles beamed.

"Oh!" Morgan clapped her hands together. "Congratulations!" She leaned forward and gave Miles a kiss before leaning down and scratching Bill behind the ears.

"And," Miles continued excitedly, "I saw Dr. Kelly in the hospital when we were doing the testing around medical equipment. He asked if Bill and I would visit some of the wounded veterans that he treats for PTSD at the hospital next week."

Morgan smiled up at Miles and took his hand in hers. "That's fantastic! I'm so proud of you for taking control of your PTSD. And I'm proud of Bill too. You two will help so many people. Now, let's celebrate! It's a good thing your mom foresaw you passing the tests. I heard she even made a special dinner just for Bill."

Morgan helped Bill into the back seat of the car as she thought of Mrs. Davies. She and Paige had made a real effort to get to know her over the last couple of months and in return Morgan had begun to feel comfortable with the entire Davies family. She had also gotten to know her own family. Morgan and Pam were close again after all these years apart. She enjoyed hanging out with her brother-in-law and her rambunctious nephews. She loved standing on the sidelines cheering at their soccer matches with Pam while Miles and Jeffery laughed at them in the bleachers.

"I have a better idea. We don't need to be at my parents until six, which means we have time for a private celebration." Miles pulled her close and she had no doubt what he meant.

Miles watched Morgan as she shimmied her black skinny jeans over her delectable behind and slid both straps of her bra over her shoulders. Miles sighed. He hated it when she got dressed again, but there was something so satisfying in being able to see all her little rituals.

"If you don't mind, I'd like to take a detour on the way to my parents' house," Miles said casually as he slid his feet into his black leather shoes.

"Sure. Where are we going?" she asked as she finished dressing.

"I just need to check on something. It won't take too long."

"Okay." Morgan chose shoes from her side of the closet in his newly repaired house and put them on. "I'm ready to go." She smiled and Miles felt his heart skip a beat. She was beautiful and she was his. He just hoped he didn't screw it up now.

Morgan rolled down her window and took a deep breath. The smell of freshly cut grass and blooming flowers drifted in. She closed her eyes and enjoyed the feel of the breeze blowing her hair.

She couldn't believe she'd been here for four months already. A part of her felt that time had gone by so fast. The other part felt as if she had never left Keeneston all those years ago. Morgan had taken her term of unemployment well. She'd used the time to become reacquainted with the town and its people. She apologized to those she had hurt and had been fully welcomed back into the fold. Now she just had to tell those that had become so close what her plans were for the future, hoping they'd be okay with it.

Morgan opened her eyes as Miles slowed the car. She looked around and saw they were on a dirt road in the middle of a field full of wildflowers. There was a herd of cows in a nearby field that Bill barked at happily.

"Oh, I know where we are. Isn't this where the infamous water tower is?" Morgan turned in her seat and saw it out the back window.

"Sure is. You don't have a paint brush on you, do you?" Miles teased as he got out of the car and walked around to open hers.

"No. I've learned my lesson. I'm walking the straight and narrow from now on!" Morgan giggled as Bill bounded around in the ankle-high grass and into a patch of wildflowers taller than him. "Now, why are we here?"

"I thought we could take a short walk before we enter the craziness of my mom's house. Besides, when we get to Mom's I'll have to leave you for my girl," Miles laced his fingers through hers and brought them up to his lips for a kiss as his eye twinkled with mischief.

Morgan laughed as she leaned against him. Little Sophie had Miles wrapped around her chubby finger. They started off through the field keeping a wide berth around the notorious water tower that now read 'KHS Football State Champions' on the far side. Bill frolicked through the field becoming a pest to some of the cows close to the fence line, but she didn't have the heart to tell him no. The little dog with the gray face was practically smiling as he went off chasing a butterfly.

The sun warmed her as they walked in comfortable silence down a small path through the beautiful flowers. Miles leaned over and picked a bunch of beautiful white daisies that were dancing in the spring breeze. Morgan smiled and reveled in her happiness as they came to a stop and Miles handed them to her. His eyes seemed to match the green of the field today.

"So, all those years ago when you vandalized the city's water tower, did you think it was romantic?" Miles asked as he slipped a beautiful deep purple flower behind her ear.

"Kinda. A part of me thought you'd finally see me and come to your senses and see how wonderful I was. The other part just wanted you to finally be in trouble with Red," Morgan teased.

"It was worth it. If you hadn't kissed me all those years ago and painted the water tower, I'd never have remembered you. Instead I've never forgotten you. You have held a place in my heart all these years." Miles paused and then shot her a killer grin, "Of course I was madder than hell at you, but you still managed to get a hold of me and never let me go. Instead, I fell in love with you and now you have my whole heart, not just one piece. I want to spend the rest of my life with you showing you how much you mean to me."

Morgan felt tears spring to her eyes. She had never thought she would hear those words from him and now here she was with his heart in her hands. However, she realized what an idiot she had been all those years ago. Morgan had thought she loved Miles, but she didn't. She didn't know the meaning of those words until now. Until Miles showed her what love was really like.

"Close your eyes, sweetheart," Miles whispered gently. Oh my God! Was he? No, he couldn't be! But it felt like he was. If she opened her eyes and he was on one knee she thought she'd faint. Instead she felt Miles turn her around. What? Was she going to pin the tail on the engagement ring?

"I've got a surprise for you," he said. She could tell he was proud of it and she could also tell he was still standing. Damn. Morgan had to admit she was slightly embarrassed for jumping the gun on the whole marriage thing. She had been thinking about it constantly, but they hadn't even discussed it. That's why she was so nervous. She was going to tell him and his family that she had decided to stay in Keeneston permanently. "Okay, open your eyes, sweetheart."

Morgan opened her eyes and saw Miles standing next to her. Double damn. Then she saw the field. The cows. Bill frolicking in the flowers. The water tower that read 'Morgan, Will You Marry Me?' The car parked… Morgan snapped her eyes back to the water tower and read it again. She was pretty sure she was imagining things until Miles dropped to one knee and pulled out a black velvet box.

"Ohhh, you're going to be in so much trouble with the sheriff," Morgan laughed through the tears starting to roll down her cheeks.

"It'll be worth it if you say you'll marry me." Tears fell faster as Morgan realized how nervous Miles really was. The box was shaking slightly as he waited for her answer.

"Yes! I'll marry you!" Morgan squealed as Miles's unsteady hands slipped the oval diamond surrounded by two purple amethysts onto her finger. "I love you!" She leapt into his arms and planned to spend the rest of her life loving this man with her whole heart.

Chapter Twenty-Five

Morgan couldn't stop staring. It was so beautiful! And how it sparkled when the light hit it. Morgan finally relinquished her hand to Miles when they had gotten in the car to head to the family dinner. He kept running his thumb over it, making sure it was really on her finger.

"I just can't believe this! I think I'm still in shock." Morgan laughed as they pulled up to the Davies farm. "Are we late?" she asked, as she looked around at all the cars already parked by the old farmhouse.

Morgan looked up at the house and found faces plastered to all the windows looking out at them. "Did you tell your parents you were going to propose?"

"Sweetheart, I asked you by painting the water tower—everyone in the county knows!" Miles laughed as he gave her hand a reassuring squeeze before getting out of the car and opening her door.

The front door to the house was thrown open and members of the Davies family poured out. Marcy pushed her way past them and hurried down the stairs to envelope Morgan in a hug. Paige, Katelyn, and Annie had to pry Marcy away to be able to welcome her to the family.

Miles was similarly surrounded by his father and brothers slapping him on the back and shaking hands. Bill danced around on his hind legs barking at the excitement in the air.

"Well," Marcy clapped her hands, "everyone get inside. We have a wedding to plan!" Marcy put Bill to shame as she used her dishtowel to herd the family inside.

"I can't believe you painted over my state championship!" Cade teased his brother.

"Attention, I have an engagement gift to present!" Marshall called out as he entered the room. "To Morgan and Miles. I wish you many years of happiness," Marshall handed his brother a large can of white paint with a red bow on it. "I'd hate to arrest you for vandalism," Marshall said with a big grin leading Morgan to think he would actually enjoy it a little.

"Well, as long as he's out in time for the bachelor party I get to plan!" Peirce rubbed his hands together and smirked. There was no doubt in Morgan's mind that she was going to hate her brother-in-law for whatever he was planning.

"I was thinking of something low key," Miles said, trying to reign in his little brother.

"Nope. You already agreed at Marshall's lame-ass party that I'd be in charge of yours when you got married. It'll be perfect! I've been planning it for the last month. Don't look at me like that," Pierce said to Miles when he had simply raised an eyebrow in disbelief. "Anyone could tell you two were going to get married."

"So, which strip club will we be attending?" Cade asked sarcastically but truthfully.

"Come on. Give me some credit will you? As soon as you all pick a wedding date, I'll pick a date for the party down at Dale Hollow Lake. We'll rent some cabins and some jet skis and cook out at night. I was going to invite all your Army buddies, so make sure to give me a list."

"Who are you?" Miles asked in disbelief.

"The brother that's going to throw you a kick-ass bachelor party, that's who."

"So, have you all set a date?" Katelyn asked.

"The sooner the better," Miles told them as he pulled Morgan close to his side.

"Well! We'd better get to work then. Ladies, to the dining room!" Marcy commanded. It was very clear to Morgan where Miles had inherited it.

"But, Ma! What about dinner?" Pierce called out.

"I daresay you boys know where the kitchen is." Marcy stopped and then turned to the living room full of hungry men. Cole was holding his baby son and Miles was already bouncing Sophie on his knee, "Oh, and make sure to make enough for us. We'll be ready for dinner by the time you have it ready. Wedding planning is hard work!"

Morgan stepped out of her shoes and unpinned her hair. They had planned the night away. Their wedding was to be in six weeks. The mid-June weather would be beautiful. Father James would marry them in the church and the reception would be held at the Davies farm. Pam had been called in and the women had sat around the large table doing more planning than Morgan ever thought possible.

Miles came up behind her wrapping his strong arms around her as he watched her in the mirror over the dresser. "I hated tonight," Miles pouted.

"Why?"

"Because those evil women kept me away from you when all I wanted to do was run my hands over your body and kiss every inch," Miles murmured as he kissed her neck.

"Miles?" Morgan asked hesitantly.

"Yes, sweetheart?"

"Do you really want me to be your wife?" She felt silly asking, but she just couldn't believe her dream was coming true.

"I can't wait to make you my wife, my love. If I could, I'd marry you tomorrow," Miles said as he slipped her shirt off her shoulder and kissed her newly exposed skin.

"If that's what you want, why don't we do that?"

His head shot up and caught her eye in the mirror. "Because I'm scared of what my mother would do!"

"A big tough man like you is afraid of his mother?" Morgan teased.

"Hell yes. She seems all sweet on the outside, but she raised five boys. Do I need to say more?"

"Good point," Morgan laughed as Miles went back to slowly undressing her. "I bet you'll be a big pushover, won't you?"

Miles tossed her bra aside with one hand as his other slipped under the waistband of her panties. Morgan gasped as his fingers found her sweet spot. His other hand came around to caress her bare breast as his mouth worked his way down her neck. "I can't wait to find out."

Morgan couldn't stop grinning as she parked her car on Main Street. Miles had left for work late this morning, an event that left her feeling inordinately proud. After a night like that, she needed pancakes.

Morgan crossed the street and smiled as the sounds and smells of the Blossom Café reached her. The patrons turned and offered their congratulations as she opened the screen door.

"I'm making a bet. In nine months the water tower will be painted either blue or pink reading, 'It's a Boy' or 'It's a Girl'. Don't you two know how to do anything privately?" Mr. Wolfe joked as he took a bite of his grits.

"Who are you kidding? Nothing is private as far as you're concerned!" Miss Daisy shot back at him to the amusement of the café.

"I guess that means you're stickin' around?" Miss Violet asked from the kitchen window. "What are you going to do now? Besides eating some of my famous pancakes," Miss Violet chuckled as she mixed the batter.

"I'm going to open my own consulting company." Morgan took a seat alone at her table although friends surrounded her.

"Don't you think she'll be a wonderful boss?" Pam asked as she walked through the door. "'Morgan Davies Consulting' sounds perfect! I'm so proud of you," Pam smiled as she took the empty seat at the table.

"Thanks Pam. That means so much to me." Morgan felt her heart grow with the support from her sister.

"The boys are so excited about being ring bearers. I must admit, I'm pretty excited about being the matron of honor too," Pam giggled as she and Morgan started talking about the wedding and her new business.

Morgan was thriving with the love and support of her sister and her fiancé. Miles had already told her that Family Farms would be her first client. She was going to work on finding a way to strengthen the company against potential takeovers. Although David was sitting in a jail cell, he had still known a good business deal when he saw it. Others would soon come knocking. She and Miles were going to work together to find a way to keep the family farms just that.

Morgan couldn't be happier. She had a fiancé that loved her, a sister that supported her, and a town that embraced her. Her real life was even better than her dreams could ever be!

Miles had finished sending the names of all his military buddies to Pierce when the direct line rang at his desk. Knowing it was Morgan, he didn't even bother to check caller ID. She had promised to give him a call and let him know when her bachelorette party would be so he could tell Pierce.

"Hey, sweetheart," Miles said as he answered the phone.

"It's nice to feel wanted," a deep voice said back to him.

"Cy! Sorry, I thought it was Morgan calling," Miles paused, all his senses kicking in. "What's the matter?"

Cy sighed into the phone, "Nothing a couple pain relievers can't take care of. I had to call and offer my congratulations. Y'all are dropping like flies."

Miles grinned. Cy wasn't the marrying type. He was the travel-all-over-the-world, girl-in-every-port type of guy. "How'd you know?"

"I could see the water tower from here!" Cy joked.

"Where is here?"

"Switzerland."

"What are you doing there?" Miles asked. Cy, with his shaved head and tattooed arm, wasn't really the Switzerland type.

"I'm skiing. Hence, the need for pain relievers."

"Do you know when you're coming home yet? You know I'd love for you to be in the wedding." Miles hoped, but knew it wasn't likely.

"Wish I could, but it doesn't look like I'll make it home. I'm sorry I'm going to miss the wedding. You know I want to be there."

"What job are you on?" Miles wondered.

"Just trying to make my way though a whole bunch of snow bunnies," Cy's gravely voice chuckled.

"You know I could find out," Miles said in all seriousness.

"I do, but you won't," Cy responded.

"Not yet. I will if I think I need to."

"I know and I know I can count on you, but I need time to make my own mark," Cy told him.

"I miss you, you know?"

"Me too. Tell everyone I love them. And try not to let Pierce get you all arrested down at the lake."

"Yeah, then I'd need your help!"

Miles talked with Cy a little longer before he heard his cell phone ring. They said their goodbyes, but he couldn't help but think something more was going on that Cy wasn't telling him. Well, hell, he knew things were going on that Cy wasn't telling him, he just didn't know what they were.

This time the caller ID on his phone showed it was Morgan calling. His dark mood lifted as he answered his phone. He never envisioned himself as a family man, but he found himself looking forward to getting home every night. Even if he didn't tell Morgan, he dreamed of little children running around his office. But first he had a wedding to go to.

Epilogue

Morgan looked in the mirror as Pam attached her fingertip lace veil. Morgan loved her dress, a lovely ivory lace gown that hugged her curves and flared into a beautiful trumpet bottom. When she walked down the aisle it looked like the bottom of her dress swirled.

"You look so beautiful!" Annie clapped her hands as she walked into the room dressed in her amethyst bridesmaid dress and carrying Morgan's bouquet of flowers.

"Oh, you're stunning!" Paige cried as she came in after Annie. "Are you ready to get married?"

"Absolutely!"

Miss Lily and her sisters took their seats in the church. Beautiful string music played as the ceremony was about to begin. Each of the sisters gave the others a grin. Only two more were left and they had a good feeling another Davies brother was going to be bit by the love bug very soon. If not, they'd just have to play cupid all on their own.

"Oh, look how handsome they all look!" Miss Lily whispered to her sisters as the Davies men came to stand at the front of the church in their tuxedos.

"Do you really think Pierce will be the next to fall?" Miss Daisy asked.

"Twenty bucks says he is," Miss Violet dug around her purse and showed the twenty to Miss Daisy.

"Deal."

The doors to the church opened and Tammy hurried in. Miss Lily felt her eyes widen at the sight of the small sprite of a girl suddenly turned into a woman. Gone were the jeans and t-shirt, replaced by a form-fitting little black dress with a plunging neckline and a pair of four-inch heels.

"Whoa. Look at that accessory," Miss Lily whispered.

"I know. Those shoes are amazing," Miss Violet replied.

"She's talking about that necklace that disappears into her cleavage," Miss Daisy told Violet.

"You're both wrong. I'm talking about him," Miss Lily pointed to the man hurrying in behind Tammy. The women all sucked in a breath as the Greek god smiled down at Tammy and slipped her hand into the crook of her arm.

"Talk about tall, dark, and sexy," Miss Daisy whistled as Tammy and her hunky man took a seat.

"He looks like an underwear model," Miss Violet said wistfully.

A whispered curse filled the church and everyone looked around to see who had said it, but then the music started and everyone turned to watch the wedding party enter. All except the Rose sisters, who saw the clenched jaw and fisted hands of Pierce Davies standing in front of the church before Cade gently nudged him and he put a smile back on his face.

Miss Daisy let out her own curse and dug around in her purse until she found what she was looking for. She handed her sister a twenty. "I guess you were right."

"Told ya," Miss Violet grinned.

Miles stood at the front of the church waiting to get a glimpse of his bride. The candles twinkled, casting a warm glow on the purple and green flowers adorning the church. The music started and Miles felt his heart speed up. The doors to the church opened and his bride was there, gliding down the aisle toward him.

Miles felt his breath leave him as a lump formed in his throat. She really was breathtaking. She smiled up at him and he felt a love he had never known before. His own little piece of trouble was going to make him the luckiest man in the world.

Before he knew it Father James told him to kiss his bride. He finally felt as if he could breathe. Some small part of him was worried the whole time that she'd refuse and he'd wake up from this dream. Miles lowered his lips to hers and kissed her with all the love he felt.

"I am happy to introduce to you for the first time, Mr. and Mrs. Miles Davies!"

About the Author

Kathleen Brooks is the bestselling author of the Bluegrass Series. She has garnered attention as a new voice in romance with a warm Southern feel. Her books feature quirky small town characters you'll feel like you've known forever, romance, humor, and mystery all mixed into one perfect glass of sweet tea.

Kathleen is an animal lover who supports rescue organizations and other non-profit organizations whose goals are to protect and save our four-legged family members.

Kathleen lives in Central Kentucky with her husband, daughter, two dogs, and a cat who thinks he's a dog. She loves to hear from readers and can be reached at Kathleen@Kathleen-Brooks.com

Check out the Website (www.kathleen-brooks.com) for updates on the Bluegrass Series. You can also "Like" Kathleen on Facebook (www.facebook.com/KathleenBrooksAuthor) and follow her on Twitter @BluegrassBrooks.

Other Books by Kathleen Brooks

Bluegrass Series

Bluegrass State of Mind

McKenna Mason, a New York City attorney with a love of all things Prada, is on the run from a group of powerful, dangerous men. McKenna turns to a teenage crush, Will Ashton, for help in starting a new life in beautiful horse country. She finds that Will is now a handsome, successful race horse farm owner. As the old flame is ignited, complications are aplenty in the form of a nasty ex-wife, an ex-boyfriend intent on killing her, and a feisty race horse who refuses to race without a kiss. Can Will and McKenna cross the finish line together, and more importantly, alive?

Risky Shot

Danielle De Luca, an ex-beauty queen who is not at all what she seems, leaves the streets of New York after tracking the criminals out to destroy her. She travels to Keeneston, Kentucky, to make her final stand by the side of her best friend McKenna Mason. While in Keeneston, Danielle meets the quiet and mysterious Mohtadi Ali Rahman, a modern day prince. Can Mo protect Dani from the group of powerful men in New York? Or will Dani save the prince from his rigid, loveless destiny?

Dead Heat

In the third book of the Bluegrass Series, Paige Davies finds her world turned upside down as she becomes involved in her best friend's nightmare. The strong-willed Paige doesn't know which is worse: someone trying to kill her, or losing her dog to the man she loves to hate.

FBI Agent Cole Parker can't decide whether he should strangle or kiss this infuriating woman of his dreams. As he works the case of his career, he finds that love can be tougher than bringing down some of the most powerful men in America.

Bluegrass Brothers Series

Bluegrass Undercover

Cade Davies had too much on his plate to pay attention to newest resident of Keeneston. He was too busy avoiding the Davies Brothers marriage trap set by half the town. But when a curvy redhead lands in Keeneston, the retired Army Ranger finds himself drawn to her. These feelings are only fueled by her apparent indifference and lack of faith in his ability to defend himself.

DEA Agent Annie Blake was undercover to bust a drug ring hiding in the adorable Southern town that preyed on high school athletes. She had thought to keep her head down and listen to the local gossip to find the maker of this deadly drug. What Annie didn't count on was becoming the local gossip. With marriage bets being placed, and an entire town aiming to win the pot, Annie looks to Cade for help in bringing down the drug ring before another kid is killed. But can she deal with the feelings that follow?

Rising Storm

Katelyn Jacks was used to being front and center as a model. But she never had to confront the Keeneston Grapevine! After retiring from the runway and returning to town to open a new animal clinic, Katelyn found that her life in the public eye was anything but over. While working hard to establish herself as the new veterinarian in town, Katelyn finds her life uprooted by a storm of love, gossip, and a vicious group of criminals.

Marshall Davies is the new Sheriff in Keeneston. He is also right at the top of the town's most eligible bachelor list. His affinity for teasing the hot new veterinarian in town has led to a rush of emotions that he wasn't ready for. Marshall finds his easy days of breaking up fights at the local PTA meetings are over when he and Katelyn discover that a dog-fighting ring has stormed into their normally idyllic town. As their love struggles to break through, they must battle to save the lives of the dogs and each other.

Bluegrass Brothers Series Continues!

The fourth book in the Bluegrass Brothers Series will be out in last spring/early summer of 2013. Be sure to like me on Facebook (www.facebook.com/KathleenBrooksAuthor) or follow my Blog (www.kathleen-brooks.blogspot.com) to get updates on the release date!

Pierce Davies has a secret… one he's kept for the past two years. But now it seems inconsequential at the sight of Tammy Fields on the arm of that Greek God. That is, until Pierce is arrested for murder. Now it's up to Tammy to save him.

Make sure you don't miss each new book as they are published. Sign up email notification of all new releases at **http://www.Kathleen-Brooks.com**.

Made in the USA
Middletown, DE
17 December 2016